COLLATERAL 2

Debt Collection #2

By Roxie Rivera

Night Works Books
3515-B Longmire Drive #103
College Station, Texas 77845
www.roxierivera.com

Publisher's Note: This is a work of fiction. Names, characters, places, and incidents are a product of the author's imagination. Locales and public names are sometimes used for atmospheric purposes. Any resemblance to actual people, living or dead, or to businesses, companies, events, institutions, or locales is completely coincidental.

COLLATERAL 2/Roxie Rivera—1st ed.

"*Te qifsha.*"

Ben laughed at the rude remark and decided to be helpful. He wandered over to the right section and plucked a Virginia Woolf title from the shelves. He brought it back to Besian and handed it to him. "Here. Read this one. It's one of Marley's favorites."

"How do you know that?" Besian took the book and flipped to the back cover.

"Because Aston has a copy in her bedroom with Marley's handwriting that says, 'One of my favorites,'" he explained matter-of-factly.

Besian whacked him with the book. "How fucking nosy are you? Going through your girlfriend's bookshelves?"

"Jesus," Ben hissed and rubbed at his stinging chest. "I'm just trying to help you."

Looking almost embarrassed, he admitted, "I'm trying to understand her." He blew out a noisy breath. "I feel like a fucking teenager again, chasing after the pretty girl in school. I have no idea what the hell I'm doing. My usual game won't work with her."

"I don't think she's the kind of girl who wants to play games," Ben said carefully.

"I know," Besian replied quietly. "I'm tired of playing games, too."

"Maybe I could ask Aston to set up a dinner or something?"

"No," Besian cut in quickly.

"It was just an idea."

"Leave the ideas to me." Besian adjusted his stack of books and asked, "How was Ags?"

"He's beat to hell, but he'll be okay."

"Did he have any information?"

Ben shook his head and decided not to say anything about Ags using the same route multiple times. "Nothing useful. Same thing Aleks told us. Red truck. Didn't see the thief's face. It's not much to go on, boss."

"No, it's not. I'm headed to a meeting with Nikolai to discuss our problem. Get out on the streets and work your contacts. Someone knows something."

"Of course, they do, but who the hell is going to be stupid enough to say something?"

"Motivate them," Besian replied, his tone cool but his meaning dark.

Not wanting to show his distaste for the violence implied, Ben schooled his features and simply nodded. "Yes, boss."

"Don't," Besian warned. "You're still part of this family. You have your girl. I gave you my blessing, but that blessing doesn't absolve you from your obligations to the family. You're an enforcer, Ben. You're *my* enforcer."

"I know exactly what I am," Ben replied. "I've always done my job, and I don't plan to stop now."

"But?"

"But I have to go to a wedding tomorrow night, and I don't want to embarrass Aston by showing up with a black eye or busted knuckles."

Besian frowned. "What wedding?"

"Her dad's best friend is getting married again. It's his fourth wife or something like that," Ben said. "He's like an uncle to her. He's running the company until she's ready to take over. They're very close."

"I wanted you to work the poker tournament tomorrow night. We need extra security."

"I can't. I promised her I would be there."

After an uncomfortably long moment, Besian said, "Fine. Go."

"I wasn't asking your permission."

"Careful, Ben," Besian warned. "We're family, but I'm your boss." Signaling the end of their discussion, Besian gestured for him to leave. "I'll be at the new club later. Find me."

"Sure thing, boss." Irritated but not at all surprised by Besian's attitude, Ben left the bookstore. He had one leg slung over his bike when Besian poked his head out the door of the bookstore and shouted, "Get a haircut before the wedding!"

Ben waved to acknowledge the order. He ran his fingers through his admittedly shaggy hair before pulling on his helmet. Maybe the boss had a point. This wedding was a high-class affair.

Deciding he would squeeze in a visit to the barber shop, he headed straight to the territory controlled by Diego Reyes. He hadn't been joking earlier that morning when he told Aston about the Reyes brothers. They were exactly as he'd described.

Although they controlled almost a quarter of Houston's underworld, they still lived with their grandmother and younger sister in the same house where they had been raised. It was a modest ranch the brothers had renovated and remodeled throughout the years. When Ben parked on the street out front, he noticed the fence had been freshly painted and the roof looked newly replaced. There roses blooming on the bushes and the grass was green and lush.

Diego's grandmother sat on her front porch with a cup of coffee and her sleek black cat nestled on her nap. He climbed off his bike and walked over to the gate. Smiling at her, he greeted, "*Buenos dias, señora. Puedo hablar con Diego?*"

"Benito!" She greeted him with a toothy smile and flicked her fingers to beckon him inside the yard. "You haven't visited in months, *mijo.*"

"I've been busy, *senora,*" he explained apologetically and closed the gate behind him. She likely knew the real reason he hadn't come to visit. He and Diego had been friends since kindergarten, but they had grown apart because of their ties to competing crime families. With all of the recent trouble with the cartel and the Hermanos street gang, it had been safer for Ben to stay away from the Reyes brothers. "How have you been?"

"Oh, you know," she said with a wave of her hand. With an amused smile, she asked, "How is Aston?"

"She's good." He was saved from a deeper interrogation by the appearance of a familiar face at the front door. "Diego."

"Ben." Diego opened the screen door and stepped onto the porch. He smiled at his grandmother and bent down to kiss her cheek. "Is this *mocoso* bothering you?"

"Benito could never bother me." She laughed as she rose to her feet, coffee in one hand and her lazy, sleepy cat in the other. "Take your jacket when you leave. It's going to rain later."

"Your knees?" Diego asked with concern.

"I'll be fine." She patted his chest and glanced back at Ben. "It was good to see you, *mijo.* You're always welcome in our house."

"It was good to see you, *senora*."

Diego held the door for his grandmother and waited until she was safely inside to turn toward Ben with a frown. "You could have called first."

"I could have."

Diego leaned back against the wall. "Is this about the robbery?"

"Yes. I'm just looking for information. You have a lot of eyes and ears on the streets now. I figured if anyone was going to have information…"

"I haven't heard anything that can help you, Ben. We have no idea who hit your crew. Hell, I don't know anyone stupid enough to steal from Besian. You'd have to be crazy to steal from someone who likes to chop off fingers."

"Someone was crazy enough to do it."

Diego shook his head. "There's no way it's anyone we know. None of the crews in town would dare. It's got to be someone outside our circle of friends."

Ben concurred. "Would have been easier to handle if it was someone running in our world."

Diego nodded in agreement. "We're ramping up our own security for obvious reasons. If someone had big enough balls to steal Besian's cash, they might be brave enough to try for ours."

"Let's hope not." Ben extended his hand, and Diego shook it. "It's good to see you."

"You, too, Ben." Diego let go. "We should get together sometime. You can bring Aston to one of my clubs."

"Your aunt would love it if we had a chaperone," he joked.

Diego laughed. "Believe me. I've heard all about you and

your bad influence on her precious little Aston." His expression turned more serious. "Tia Nina loves Aston like her own kid. She's been with the family since Aston was born. She cares about her, and she will not hesitate to send us after you."

"Duly noted," Ben said with a nod. Backing away, he said, "I'll see you around, Diego."

"Stay safe, Ben."

"You, too."

With his first contact crossed off his list, Ben slung his leg over his bike and pulled his helmet into place. The bike roared to life beneath him. Only seven more to go…

CHAPTER THREE

"A STON, THERE'S A detective waiting for you in the conference room."

Taken aback by Betty's unusual greeting, I lowered my sunglasses and tucked them into my handbag. "A detective? Here to see me?"

Betty glanced anxiously at the conference room located just off the front reception of the accounting and finance floor. "He was waiting when I got here. I put him in the conference room and gave him coffee. I didn't want him alone at your desk. I thought he might snoop."

"Thank you, Betty." Worried something had happened to Ben, I walked quickly toward the conference room, knocked on the closed door and stepped inside. Putting on my best professional smile, I greeted the man standing on the other side of the room. "Hello. Betty said you wanted to speak with me?"

"Miss McNeil, I'm Detective Shaw." He shifted his coffee cup to the other hand before offering a handshake. Tall and broad shouldered, he looked like a linebacker but had a genuine smile that put me at ease.

"Aston is fine," I said, taking his hand and shaking it. Gesturing to the table, I took a seat and waited for him to sit.

"What can I do for you this morning?"

Please, please, don't let it be Ben.

"I'm here to ask you some questions about your brother," Detective Shaw explained as he took a small notebook and a pen from the inner pocket of his suit jacket.

"Calvin is my stepbrother," I said on reflex. The thought of him being a blood relative sickened me. I wanted absolutely no connections to him, not in life and certainly not in death.

"Right. Sorry." He clicked the pen twice before scribbling on his notebook. "When was the last time you saw Calvin?"

The night he tried to kill me.

"It's been a few weeks," I answered vaguely. "We aren't close so we don't have much contact."

"I read his juvenile records," Detective Shaw said, his eyes gentle. "I don't blame you for not wanting to spend much time with him."

"He is a difficult person," I agreed, silently reminding myself to talk about him as if he were still alive. "Is he in trouble?"

"He might be," the detective replied. "He was involved in some shady financial business and quite a few of his associates have gone missing."

"Missing? Like...dead?"

"It's possible." He reached into his pocket and withdrew a sheet of paper with photos printed on it. "Do you recognize any of these men?"

I pulled the wrinkled sheet of paper closer and studied the faces printed on it. There didn't seem to a common thread among any of the men on it. Young. Old. Latino. White. Asian. "I don't recognize any of them."

"You sure?"

Wondering if I was supposed to recognize someone on the page, I gave it a closer look. There was one face that looked vaguely familiar. "This guy maybe." I tapped the photo of a smiling man in a collared shirt. "I feel like I've seen him somewhere."

"He's married to one of your coworkers."

"I must have seen him at one of our holiday parties or the Fourth of July picnic," I murmured, trying to place him. "What's his name?"

"Gary Metcalf."

"Metcalf? Oh! Margie's husband! Yeah. I've met him once? Maybe twice? He seemed like a nice guy."

"He is," Detective Shaw said. "I think he may have gotten in over his head."

"With Calvin?" I tried to piece together the few clues the detective had given me. "I don't see how their paths would have crossed."

"We think they got to know each other over some real estate deals." He tucked the sheet of photos back in his pocket. "Do you know where Calvin has been living? We checked his last known address, but he was evicted from the penthouse three weeks ago."

"I have no idea where he is," I answered, telling the absolute truth. Whatever happened to Calvin after Ben's friend dragged him out of my house was a mystery to me.

"Does he travel often?"

"He does."

"To Asia?"

"Yes, actually," I confirmed, thinking of all the trips he had taken there over the years."

"He spends a lot of time in Macau and Hong Kong. Any reason he likes those areas?"

"If I had to guess? Gambling."

"Why do you say that?"

"He got into a mess there a few years ago. Back when his mom was alive," I clarified. "My dad and stepmom had to fly out in the middle of the night to handle it. I knew better than to ask any questions so I'm not sure of the details."

"Do you know if he has access to money? Bank accounts? Safety deposit boxes? Stocks? Things he could sell?"

"He has an inheritance. How much of it he has left? I couldn't tell you."

"How much was in the inheritance?"

"I'm not sure."

"Millions?"

"Yes. Less than ten," I added, thinking of the financial paperwork I had come across after my father's death. "His mother left him some life insurance policies, some stock and a few pieces of commercial real estate. As far as I know, he liquidated everything in the trust when he gained control."

As I answered the detective's questions, I started to piece things together for myself. Real estate. Was that how he had met Gary Metcalf? Had Gary been involved in selling the real estate?

"Well, if he's been evicted, I'm going to guess that he's flat broke," the deputy reasoned. "Could he come to you for money?"

"He could," I said carefully.

"But?"

"He won't."

"Because?"

"Because he knows I'm not going to give him a dime," I explained.

"And this place?" He gestured around the room. "Could Calvin get money from here?"

"No. This was my father's business, and he was very careful to exclude Calvin from every part of it."

"The Limestone Group." He grabbed one of the brochures in the center of the conference table and thumbed through it. "What exactly is a private equity firm? It's investments, right?"

"Yes."

"You buy businesses?"

"Sometimes, yes."

"And you make money off of that?"

"We take money from investors and buy businesses that are struggling but have untapped value. We fix them up, hold onto them for a few years and then sell them at a profit."

"Can't be that easy," he said, a knowing gleam in his eye.

"No, it's definitely not," I agreed. "Sometimes we get the analysis wrong and buy into something that is unsalvageable. At that point, the firm puts the business into bankruptcy as quickly as possible and tries to squeeze whatever money we can out of it."

"And the workers?"

They get shafted. I couldn't say that, of course. "We provide the workers with training and access to employment firms to help them find new jobs. We have a very successful track record in securing employment for former employees of businesses we've closed."

"Uh-huh," he said in an unbelieving tone.

I shrugged. "That's the company line."

"I bet it is," he grumbled and returned the brochure to its stack. "Do you have locations overseas?"

"Europe."

He gave me an expectant look. "Specifically?"

"London is the headquarters of our branch there. It's called StrateCore. It provides logistics and planning and office spaces for various companies in the Euro zone. There's a new branch opening in Belgium soon."

"But nothing in Asia?"

"Offices? No. We have investments in Asia, and we sold a small stake in the firm to the CIC. That's the extent of our Asian presence."

"CIC?"

"It's the sovereign wealth fund for China."

"Uh-huh," he said. "And what do you do here?"

"I'm a junior analyst. Very junior," I emphasized. "I'm still working on my master's degree."

"On the job training is the best way to get a handle on any profession," he said. "We train our detectives that way. Work your way up from the bottom, you know? It makes for better investigators."

"I'm sure it does."

"Where are you going to school?"

"U of H," I answered, wondering why he was suddenly so interested in what I did.

"The evening program? My kid is thinking about it for his MBA."

"It's a good program. I'm very happy with the pace and content." I decided to keep my answers a bit more professional, just in case. I didn't want to slip up and make a mistake.

The detective flipped to the back of his notebook and removed a business card. He slid it toward me. "If you happen to hear from Calvin, please contact me as soon as possible. It's better if you don't let him know you've spoken to me."

"You don't have to worry about that." I took the card and slipped it into my purse.

"And please don't say anything to your coworker, Mrs. Metcalfe," he asked. "This was a private conversation, and I'd like to keep it that way. For her safety," he added, pinning me in place with a heavy look.

"My lips are sealed." The last thing I wanted was for Margie to get hurt. She had only just come back from maternity leave for her baby boy Elliot and didn't need any added stress.

"You might not want to tell your boyfriend I was here either," he suggested.

Confused, I frowned at him. "Why in the world would I hide this from Ben?"

Detective Shaw held my gaze for a moment. He seemed to be trying to get a read on me. Was he trying to decide if I was really that naïve? "You know what he does, don't you?"

"Ben is a small business owner. He's a mechanic. That's what he does."

He narrowed his eyes a fraction, but I cut him off before he could say anything else. Glancing at my watch, I made a face. "I'm sorry, but I have an appointment scheduled. Can I walk you out?"

"No need." He stood and held out his hand. "It was nice to meet you, Miss McNeil."

"And you, Detective Shaw."

I led him out of the conference room and watched him get on the elevator. After the doors closed, Betty turned to me with a worried expression. "Is everything okay, hon?"

"He just wanted to ask some questions about Calvin."

"Of course." Betty rolled her eyes. Then, leaning closer, she added, "You know there was another investigator here yesterday. She came in after you left for class. She was looking for Margie."

"Margie? Why?" My heart skipped in my chest. It couldn't be a coincidence that the two of us had been questioned just hours apart.

Betty shrugged. "She didn't say. They went into Margie's office for a few minutes. After the agent left, Margie rushed out of here like her hair was on fire."

"Agent? Not a detective?"

"The lady flashed a badge from the FBI!" Betty exclaimed in a stage whisper.

"Why would the FBI be investigating Margie?" My stomach clenched. Was the whole firm under investigation?

"No, no, no," Betty assured me. "I think it has to something to do with Gary."

"Gary?"

"Her husband."

"I know he's her husband. I meant—why would the FBI be investigating him? Isn't he in real estate?"

"He handles investment property funds. Something to do with 1031 exchanges," she added offhandedly. "I heard Margie calling him before the elevator doors closed. She was crying and yelling."

"That's not good."

"Men," Betty said with a sigh. "They're all trouble."

I couldn't disagree with that. "Sometimes, it's the fun kind, though."

She laughed and patted my back before answering the ringing phone. I gave her a little wave and made my way to my desk. Although I had embraced the firm's decision to get rid of cubicles and open up the main areas of each floor, I suddenly found the lack of privacy irritating.

Ignoring the interested looks of my coworkers, I fished my iPhone out of my purse and opened the last text I had shared with Ben. My thumbs hovered over the screen as I debated what to tell him. A nagging worry left me feeling unsettled. What if my phone was being tracked by the police? What if they were tapping my phone or had a subpoena for my text messages or email?

Although Ben and I hadn't been dating very long, we had already had a few deep conversations about what to do if the police came sniffing around after Calvin. There were only four of us who knew what had happened that night—me, Ben, Marley and Devil. Marley, my best friend in the whole world, would never say a word. She had been raised on the fringes of the criminal underworld and understood the stakes. Devil was part of Ben's crime family and had taken a blood oath to never hurt the family. As long as I kept my mouth shut, no one would ever know where Calvin really was.

Deciding I couldn't risk it, I chose not to say anything to Ben about the detective's visit. Instead, I sent a message letting him know I had gotten to work and reminding him about dinner. Not expecting an immediate response, I tucked my phone back in my purse and stowed it in the bottom drawer of my desk.

Finally settling into work, I opened my email and noticed the generic out of office message from Margie. Even though I was burning up with curiosity, I didn't reply to it. The last thing she needed was her work inbox jammed with nosy messages or her phone going crazy with alerts while she was trying to handle personal business.

"Everything okay?" Jed, the head analyst and my current mentor asked as he stopped at my desk.

"Yes," I said, smiling up at him. "Just a detective who wanted to speak with my stepbrother."

Jed made a face. "Is Calvin even allowed on this property? After the picnic fight?"

I cringed at the memory of Calvin attacking my father and Oliver, our current CEO, at the family picnic the firm hosted every summer. "No, he's still banned. He won't show his face here."

"Let's hope not," Jed remarked, his distaste for Calvin clear. "How's the studying for your Series 82 coming along? You having any problems?"

"No. The study guide is straight forward. I feel pretty confident about the exam."

"Good. What are you working on today?"

"I'm digging into some financial reports for Roberta."

"When you finish those, come by my office. I'd like you to work with me on a deal I'm putting together."

I didn't even try to suppress the smile that overwhelmed me. "Really?"

"Yes. Really," he said with a laugh. "You're the one who gave me the idea."

"Oh?"

"India."

"Oh!" It had been a little seedling of an idea I had thrown out during a brainstorming lunch a few weeks ago. By chance, I had been talking to a guy in my cohort who had grown up in Bangalore. My curiosity about the city had sent me down an internet rabbit hole that eventually led me to a struggling but promising office park that looked like something the firm could buy and grow into something really big and profitable.

"You have good instincts. Just like your dad," he added with a fond look. "You're ready to start working on some bigger projects. We promised your dad we would mentor you and help you reach your full potential. It's time for the next step."

"Okay. Thank you." After Jed left, I couldn't stop smiling. The pride I felt in earning my place at my father's firm filled me with such happiness. Working here, walking the same halls and sitting in the same rooms he had, helped me keep the connection alive. I missed him so very much, and I hoped that he would be proud of me now, of the hard work and extra hours I put into my job. Disappointing him or tarnishing his legacy was the very last thing I wanted.

The very real possibility that the ugly business with Calvin could do just that wiped the smile right off my face. No matter how many times Ben assured me that no one would ever find out what had really happened to Calvin, I would never truly believe it. There was always a possibility that someone else knew what had happened.

What if Devil had been seen? What if Calvin had told someone where he was going? What if he had a partner who suspected something? What if someone found the body?

I could just imagine Calvin's sadistic glee at my predica-ment. It was almost as if he had planned this eventual outcome. Even in death, he was still tormenting me. Even in death, he was going to win.

But I couldn't let him win. It wasn't only me at risk. Ben and Marley, the two people who meant the most to me in the whole world, would be hurt if the truth were ever uncovered. I couldn't let that happen. I *wouldn't* let that happen.

Whatever the cost, Calvin and the secrets that he had tak-en with him had to stay buried.

CHAPTER FOUR

SURROUNDED BY THE sound of pneumatic tools and loud music, Ben focused on the notepad in front of him as he tried to decipher Devil's shit handwriting. He tried to make sense of the customer's complaint. "Dev!"

Across the shop, Devil looked away from the Chevy he was standing under and shouted, "What?"

Ben waved the ticket. "The fuck does this say? The car does *what* at red lights?"

He smirked, his burned skin stretching taut. "Dances the cha-cha."

"What?"

"Dances the cha-cha," Devil said, swiveling his jean-clad hips in an outrageous way that made Ben instantly uncomfortable.

"Fucking stop that now," Ben ordered as the other guys in the shop laughed.

Devil shrugged his wide shoulders and reached for another tool. "That's what the old broad said. That's what I wrote down. It's the transmission."

Shaking his head, Ben entered what the customer had said into the shop computer. Reading farther down the ticket, he spotted Devil's diagnosis of transmission issues and finished inputting all the parts and labor costs to compile an estimate.

"The car dances the cha-cha," he muttered, thinking of all the crazy shit customers said when dropping off their vehicles. He waited for the estimate to print and set it aside for Jeannie to handle when she got back from her lunch break. He picked up the next ticket and glanced at the writing, this time from Jet. It was even worse than Devil's. Loudly, he announced, "I'm going to start a remedial handwriting class for you lazy ass bastards!"

"It's a miracle most of them can read," Besian remarked as he strode into the shop. "Don't push your luck with handwriting."

Ben glanced back at Besian. "Let me finish this ticket, and we'll talk?"

Besian nodded and made the rounds of the shop, stopping to speak with some of the mechanics he had known for years. Ben printed out the estimate and put it in the pile waiting for Jeannie before heading into his office and dropping into the chair behind his desk. Besian followed a few minutes later, closing the door behind him and sitting on the empty chair across from Ben.

"I talked to everyone I could think of," Ben said. "No leads. You?"

Besian shook his head. "Nothing."

Ben opened the top drawer of his desk and grabbed the pack of gum he kept stowed there. "Have you had a chance to talk to Kostya?"

"Not yet," Besian said, gesturing for Ben to hand him some gum. "I'm seeing him later. I'll ask if one of his little spiders can hack into any security or traffic cameras around the crash site."

"It was a small game, at least." Ben tried to find something to cheer up the boss.

"Sixty-seven grand," Besian answered with a long sigh. He winced and rubbed the spot where he had been shot months earlier. "It won't ruin us. It barely hurts us. Financially," he clarified. "But it's a black eye and an embarrassment. We can't even keep our money safe. How the fuck do we convince our clients that we can keep them safe while gambling with us?"

"It's one theft. *One.* In all the years you've been running the gambling scene in town, you've never had a problem like this. People know you. They trust you. You're the only high-end game in town. The only game with real money. What are your clients going to do? Travel to Vegas? The casinos in Louisiana?"

"They might," Besian insisted stubbornly.

"They won't." Ben flicked his balled-up gum wrapper into the trashcan. "I talked to Devil about changing up our routes and drivers. We'll be on alert."

"Make sure our guys aren't trigger happy. The last thing we need is someone getting shot accidentally."

"I'll relay your concerns."

"I doubt we'll get hit again," the boss said, his fingers tapping against his knee. "If this is the start of some kind of spree, the robbers will hit another outfit. They'll know we're going to step up security."

"That was my thinking, too."

"Of course, that brings other problems," Besian continued. "If the robbers are targeting people like us," he gave Ben a look, "we'll draw police interest. That's not good for anyone.

It's terrible for all of our businesses."

"Hopefully, it was just a one-time thing." Ben didn't want to even imagine how dangerous the streets would get if a robbery crew started hitting the underworld.

Besian gestured toward Ben's head. "You didn't get your hair cut."

"I was busy all morning trying to track down your money. We're slammed out in the shop." He reached up to touch the long ends of his hair. "I'll get it done."

"Where is the wedding?"

"The Bell Tower."

"Very nice place," Besian remarked. "You love this girl."

Ben nodded. "Yes."

"So, don't embarrass her tomorrow," Besian counseled. "If you need to brush up on your etiquette, go see Alina. She'll make sure you know which fork to use first and what conversation topics are safe. These high-class weddings are all about image. If you look the part, people will think you belong there."

It wasn't a bad idea. "I haven't seen Alina in a few weeks. I owe her a visit," Ben admitted, feeling a bit guilty for not carving out time for his surrogate mother.

"She'll be happy to see you. She'll want to hear all about your girl."

Ben made a face. He hadn't told anyone, especially not Aston, but he had discovered her father had once been a client of Alina's. It had been an accident, his discovery, but now that he knew, it made him uncomfortable. "Alina's going to worry about me moving too fast with Aston."

Besian regarded him for a moment. "Do you think you're

moving too fast?"

"No," he answered immediately. "It feels right. All of it."

Besian seemed to hesitate before asking, "Do you remember what you told me? About not being careful with her?"

Ben remembered. He had confessed to not using protection during their first night together. "She wasn't pregnant."

"Good. Wrap it up," Besian ordered. "Don't shame your mother by knocking up this girl before she has a ring on her finger and your last name."

Ben shifted uneasily at the thought of shaming his late mother. She had been a single mom, abandoned by his father and left to fend for herself. He would never do that to any woman he dated. Before she had died, he had promised her that he would be a good husband and father. He intended to keep that promise.

"She may not want my last name," Ben pointed out, wanting to see how the boss would react to that.

"She has to," Besian insisted.

Ben laughed. "You need to read those books you bought earlier. You're going to be shocked when you find out that some women don't. Hell, some men take the last names of their wives."

"The fuck they do," Besian grumbled and checked his watch. Standing up, he said, "I have a meeting at the bank."

"What are you buying now?"

Besian smirked. "That's my secret."

Ben scoffed. "Keep your secrets. I have enough of my own to carry."

"Stop putting your phone on silent at night," Besian ordered as he reached for the door. "Jet couldn't reach you this morning. I was—we—were worried."

Ben noticed the quick correction. Ever since his shooting, the boss had been slightly more open with his feelings. It was uncomfortable for most of the crew. They weren't exactly the most emotionally well-adjusted men.

"Check in with me later."

"Yeah." Ben didn't follow him out. He stayed at his desk and glared at his list of tasks that still needed to be complete. His stomach growled, reminding him that he had skipped breakfast. Hungry, he left his office and sought out Devil who had finished his job on the Chevy. "You hungry?"

"Always," Devil rasped. "What do you want?"

"Pho?"

"Sure." Devil gestured with his dirty hands toward his toolbox. "Let me finish up. I'll drive."

Ben spotted Jeannie returning from her lunch break and joined her at the workstation where she had paused to gather up the invoices. In her usual grandmotherly way, she asked him if he had eaten lunch yet and then all but shooed him out the door, reminding him that she had managed her husband's shop for forty years and could handle this one for an hour. He swiped his sunglasses from the top of his toolbox and walked out to Devil's truck.

As he waited, he checked his phone for any new messages from Aston. She hadn't sent anything since letting him know she'd gotten to work. That wasn't unusual on days where she was busy. Even so, he was deflated by the sight of his empty inbox.

"Usual place?" Devil asked as he unlocked the truck with his key fob.

"Yeah." Ben tucked his phone back into his pocket and got into the front passenger seat.

"What did the boss want?" Devil pulled out of his parking spot and headed for the nearest side street.

"Following up on the robbery," Ben said. "He doesn't have any leads either."

"I don't think we'll ever find them." Devil paused at a blinking yellow before turning left. "Anyone stupid enough to hit us is going to be very quiet about it."

"If they're smart," Ben agreed.

"But?"

"I don't know." He scratched at an oil stain on his jeans. "I don't think the people who robbed us are done yet."

"Why?"

"They didn't even get seventy grand. That's not very much money, not compared to the risk. You hit someone us like us? You do it because you're desperate and you need big money fast." He shook his head. "I have a feeling the people who hit us need more cash."

"Everyone in this town needs more cash," Devil grumbled. "Except you."

Ben frowned. "Aston's money is hers."

"For now."

"Forever," he countered. "I'm not interested in her money."

"Everyone is interested in her money."

"Not me."

Devil shot him a look as they idled at a red light. Finally, he said, "No, not you."

"Fucking right," Ben growled. He didn't like having his

motives questioned when it came to Aston. He especially didn't care to be compared to any of the assholes who wanted to use her for the perks of her wealth. If she lost everything tomorrow, he wouldn't love her any less. He'd live in a cardboard box under a fucking bridge with her.

They didn't talk as Devil pulled into a parking space in the lot of the rundown strip mall where Phan's, their favorite noodle shop, was located. Not a word was said as they walked into the restaurant and waited in line to order at the busy counter. He got his usual—a No. 1 *dac biet*—and moved up to the register to pay. Devil shouldered him out of the way, pulling out his wallet and paying for their meal. Ben recognized it as his friend's way of making amends for the shit he had talked in the truck.

They found two seats near the windows at the front of the shop. Ben had just cracked apart his chopsticks when he heard squealing wheels. He glanced out the floor to ceiling window just in time to see a red truck heading right for the column outside. Jumping to his feet, he grabbed a handful of Devil's shirt and jerked him toward the floor.

Screams of terror echoed in the small noodle shop as the truck slammed into the column and then through the window. Glass exploded all around them. The building shuddered and seemed to be crashing down around them. Somehow, they ended up beneath a table that protected them from the worst of it.

Breathing hard and coughing on the dust filling the air, Ben winced at the nonstop horn blaring into the restaurant. The sounds of crying and shouting filled the air. Soaked in burning hot broth, he wiped at his face and chest. He looked at

Devil and cursed under his breath when he saw the stream of blood running down his friend's face. "You're bleeding."

"No shit?" Devil replied sarcastically. "Are you—"

Gunshots interrupted him. Ben threw his hands over his head and tried to make himself as small as possible on the floor. Screams. Gunshots. It was one gun at first—short cracks—and then two guns returning fire. Zastava. He recognized the two guns answering with sharp bursts of fire. There were crates of M88s coming into Houston, most of them funneled out of Serbia. He had one in his nightstand and another as a throwaway he kept at the shop, just in case.

Was it someone from their crew shooting up the place? Was it the Russians? What the hell was happening out there?

There was a pause in the gunfire and then two loud blasts from a shotgun. A few seconds later, tires squealed as a vehicle peeled out of the parking lot. Ben waited a few heartbeats before climbing to his feet. He shifted the table out of the way and helped Devil stand. "You okay?"

"Yeah." Devil wiped the blood out of his eyes with his bare hand and rubbed the blood on his jeans.

Ben's gaze settled on the red truck now sitting in the restaurant. Was this *the* red truck? The same one from the robbery?

A pained cry tore his attention away from the truck. Heart thumping with adrenaline, Ben stumbled over to the nearest overturned table and helped an older woman off the floor. Blood seeped out of a gash in her leg. After helping her into a chair, he grabbed a handful of napkins and pressed them onto the woman's leg. Behind him, Devil mirrored his actions, helping an old man who had been trapped under a table and half a pane of broken glass. Other patrons who could still move were following suit.

At the sound of sirens, Ben caught Devil's gaze. The other man grimaced. For a brief moment, Ben wondered if they could climb over the truck and escape without being noticed. He didn't want to deal with the police, especially not if that truck was the same one from the robbery, but there was no way out. More importantly, he couldn't abandon the old lady who now gripped his hand for support.

"Please don't leave me," she pleaded, her voice soft and wavering. "Please."

"You're going to be okay," Ben promised her and added another layer of napkins to the makeshift trauma dressing. "I'm not going anywhere."

As police poured into the destroyed restaurant, Ben spotted none other than Detective Eric Santos at one of the broken windows. Grimacing, he turned his attention back to the bleeding leg and grabbed another handful of napkins. He and Eric had history that went back years and none of it was particularly good.

What the hell else could go wrong today?

CHAPTER FIVE

"I'M SURE HE'S on his way," I said, glancing at my phone for the hundredth time. Across the kitchen, Nina frowned at the stove where the incredible dinner she had made waited. Pedro sat in his usual chair at the cozy breakfast nook where we ate most of our meals together. He nursed his bottle of beer and kept his gaze glued to his Kindle to avoid the tension.

"You said that twenty minutes ago," Nina reminded me.

"Five more minutes," I pleaded. "Please?"

Nina sighed but nodded. "Five minutes."

I wasn't annoyed with Ben's tardiness. I was worried. He always updated me with texts, and I hadn't heard from him since before lunch. My mind went back to the robbery, and I couldn't stop imagining all the horrible things that might have happened to him while chasing down the money.

The deep rumble of a motorcycle eased my worries. I glanced at Nina, but her lips were pursed with discontent. It was clear she would have been happier if he hadn't come. She would have had another reason to dislike him and more ammunition for pushing me to reconsider our relationship.

When Ben walked into the kitchen a short time later, my jaw dropped. His jeans and grey work shirt were stained with blood and dirt and some kind of white dust. He had scratches on his face and neck and one of his hands was bandaged. He looked so tired and defeated.

"Ben!" I rushed to him, crossing the distance between us in a few quick strides. "What happened?"

"There was an accident," he said, his voice low and tired.

"At the shop?"

"No, at Phan's."

"The noodle shop?" He had taken me there a few times because he swore it was the best pho in town. "What kind of accident?"

"A truck drove through the front windows. Devil and I were lucky."

"Lucky?" I looked him over again. "Ben, you have blood all over you."

"It's not mine." He glanced down as if seeing it for the first time. "It's Mrs. Võ's."

"Who is Mrs. Võ?"

"She's the old lady who was sitting behind us. She got hit with a piece of glass and a table."

Touching his cheek, I asked, "Is she okay?"

He nodded. "I went with her to the hospital. Her daughter came to sit with her before I left. She needed stitches, but she'll be fine."

"That's good," I remarked, not knowing what else to say.

"Ben, *mijo*," Nina interjected gently, "you should go take a shower. You'll feel better once you're clean." Her gaze fell to his bloody clothes. "If you leave those in the laundry room, I can treat them."

Ben shook his head. "I'll throw them away."

"If you're sure…?"

"I'm sure." He leaned down and kissed my forehead. "I'll hurry. You guys should go ahead and eat."

"We'll wait," Nina said.

Surprised by her sudden turnaround, I shot her a questioning look as Ben disappeared upstairs.

"What?" she asked, almost defensively.

"Uh, you're being nice to him?"

"I'm always nice to him," she replied, her feathers obviously ruffled.

I looked at Pedro who just shrugged. "Really?"

"I'm always nice to everyone who comes into this house," she insisted. Busying herself with dishing out food onto plates, she admitted, "I like Ben. He's a good boy, but he's not the right boy for you."

"None of the guys I've dated since high school have been the right boy for me," I countered. "You've seriously hated all of them."

"I didn't hate them. I just have higher standards for you."

"We want you to be happy but also safe," Pedro finally said. "You're like a child to us. We don't want one of our kids getting tangled up with the Albanian mafia."

"I don't want it either." That was the truth. I didn't want anything to do with Ben's criminal ties. "But Ben is who he is. He was born into that family. It's a complicated issue."

"Complicated, yes," Pedro agreed, "but dangerous."

I wanted to point out that their own nephews were just as dangerous as Ben, maybe even more if the stories about Diego were true. Even so, I kept my mouth shut. I didn't want to turn this into a tit-for-tat argument. I loved Nina and Pedro and wanted them in my life, even if they were a bit overprotective.

I was a lucky girl to have two people who loved me so much.

We let the discussion drop. I joined Nina at the stove and ferried plates to the table. Ben returned, freshly showered and changed into a pair of black gym shorts and a Markovic MMA t-shirt. As soon as we sat down, Nina started a prayer. I glanced at Ben who gave me a soft look before taking my hand under the table and giving it a squeeze. As far as I knew, he wasn't particularly religious, but he respectfully bowed his head until Nina was finished.

"Where do you go to church?" Nina asked even before we had taken a single bite.

I groaned inwardly, but Ben answered without hesitation. "I don't."

"What? Never?"

He shook his head. "Never."

"What did you do on Easter? Or Christmas?"

He shrugged and tucked into his meal. "What everyone does, but without the church part."

She looked at me as if to say, "See what I mean?"

"I'm not opposed to going," he added, "if Aston wants me to go with her."

She perked up at that. "Aston, hasn't been to Mass in a few weeks." She didn't have to say I hadn't gone because I had been spending my weekends with him. "You should both come with me next week."

I shot him a perturbed look and fought the urge to kick him under the table. He smiled back in the most infuriatingly handsome way.

"Was your mother Christian?" Nina asked, still fishing for information.

"No. She wasn't religious."

"And your father?"

"He was Muslim, I think."

Nina looked like she was about to choke on her mouthful of *sopa*. She swallowed slowly and took a drink of her iced tea. Eventually, she asked, "Were you close to your dad?"

"No," he answered shortly. "We weren't close."

She seemed to understand that she had touched on a sore spot. Before she could start asking more invasive questions, Pedro changed the conversation. "Ben, how handy are you with smaller engines? I couldn't get the mower to start this morning. I'm having problems with my trimmer, too."

"Gas powered?"

Pedro nodded, and they started talking about engine repair and tools. Relieved to have the focus off Ben's family and religion, I enjoyed the rest of my dinner. Conversation flowed easily after that and centered mostly on their upcoming trip to San Antonio to visit their grandkids.

"I'll take a look at the mower and trimmer while you're gone," Ben promised as helped clear the table.

My first instinct was to recommend buying new equipment, but Ben and Pedro shared the idea that all things could be fixed. They probably wouldn't ever admit to being environmentalists, but they sure had green thoughts about reusing and upcycling.

"What time are you leaving?" I asked Nina while helping her store leftovers in the refrigerator.

"Seven," she said, stowing a container on a shelf. "We're meeting the kids for brunch."

After hugging them and wishing them well on their trip,

Ben and I turned off the lights and headed upstairs. He dropped down on my bed and fell onto his back, covering his tired eyes with his forearm. Even though I had a thousand questions about his day, I decided to give him a little space to decompress.

Closed off in the bathroom, I stripped down and turned on the shower. I put my hair up in a bun so I would have good second-day hair for the wedding tomorrow. Ben liked to tease me about my shampoo schedule, but he didn't understand the struggle.

I took a short shower and stepped out to find Ben brushing his teeth at the right sink on the double vanity, the one he had claimed for himself. More and more of his things were migrating to my place. First, it had been a handful of toiletries and an extra shirt and jeans. Now, he had full sets of clothing hanging in my closet and a drawer and shelf I'd set aside for his things.

It wasn't as if space was a problem. Lately, I had been feeling as if there was too much space. The house had always been too big. Now, it felt so empty and cold. It was an elegant house, all marble and gleaming wood with huge entertaining spaces and landscaping that rivaled the best country clubs— but it didn't feel like a home. More than once, I had gotten the distinct feeling that was I living in a mausoleum. I was stuck in this place that held so many memories of my childhood, of my family. But they were all gone. It was just me and sometimes Ben and Nina and Pedro.

Maybe it was time to let the house go.

Maybe it was time to start a new chapter of my life in a place that was free from old memories.

Wrapped in my towel, I joined him at the double vanity. I bumped his hip with mine and smiled at him before grabbing my toothbrush. His earlier fatigue seemed to have passed. Leaning forward with his hands planted on the white marble, he watched me go through my night routine of serums and creams.

"Do you want to talk about the noodle shop?" I caught his gaze in the mirror.

"It was a shit show." Ben picked up the bottle I had just put down and scrutinized the back of it. "What the hell is niacinimide?"

"It's a Vitamin B thing. Don't try to distract me. What actually happened?"

"A crew out of Nickel Jackson's territory was chasing down two guys in a red truck. Apparently, the red truck had hit one of their stash houses. One of the guys was shot and bleeding out in the passenger seat when the driver lost control and hit the restaurant. There was a shootout—"

"What!" I stopped rubbing my face and looked at him. "Were they shooting at you?"

"No." He put down the bottle and moved to stand behind me. His warm, strong hands settled on my shoulders, and he bent down to kiss the curve of my neck. "I wasn't at risk."

"A bunch of idiots were shooting each other right in front of you."

"They weren't trying to shoot me. They were too busy popping off rounds at each other."

"Did they hit their marks?"

"The driver of the red truck killed the two guys from Nickel's crew. He stole their car and took off before the police got there. Left the cash and drugs he had stolen from the stash house with his dead friend."

"That's awful."

Ben nodded and kissed my neck again. "It's worse than awful."

"Because it's gang stuff?"

"All the bosses will have to meet later tonight to keep the peace."

"Do you know who was driving the red truck?"

"No idea."

"The dead friend?"

"I've never seen him before," Ben said, his fingertips grazing my shoulder. "A detective from the gang unit was on the scene. He recognized me and had a car waiting at the hospital to take me down to the station for questioning. He's such a pain in the ass."

A worrying thought occurred to me. "Was the shooting connected to your robbery?"

Reluctantly, Ben nodded. "It was the same truck. Probably same two guys."

"Shit." The mention of police questioning made me think of my own run-in with Detective Shaw. "Ben, we need to talk about something."

"Later," he murmured, giving me a smoldering look. He tugged at the towel and let it drop around my feet. "You're so fucking beautiful, Aston."

"But, Ben," I protested weakly, wanting to tell him about the detective but also not wanting him to stop kissing and touching me.

"Later," he repeated and palmed my bottom with one of

his big hands. "I have something better to do with my mouth than talk."

I shuddered as Ben pushed me forward until I was bent over the counter. The marble was cold against my skin, and I hissed at the shock of it. Covering my body with his, Ben kissed his way down my spine. His erection pressed against my bottom, giving me a promise of what was to come.

"I thought about you all day." His rough hands set my skin on fire as he caressed me with appreciative strokes. "I feel like I'm always sneaking in late and running out early. I'm not spending enough time with you."

"Ben, you give me what you can." I shivered as he sucked on my neck. "We're both so busy. Any time we spend together is precious to me."

"That's why I'm not wasting my chance for this." He pulled off his shirt and threw it aside. I let my hungry gaze roam his reflection, taking in his broad chest and the ripple of his muscles. A moment later, he sank to his knees behind me. His hand settled on the small of my back, pushing me down flat. He gripped my hips and canted them up before pushing my thighs apart and stunning me with a long lick.

"Ben!"

He laughed darkly and stabbed his tongue between my labia. He seemed to enjoy shocking me with things like this. Not that I was complaining. He might do the dirtiest things to me—but they felt so good. Sinfully good.

He pushed my thighs even farther apart and attacked me with his mouth. The sensations were so strong I tried to wiggle away, but he pulled me back, holding onto my thighs and anchoring me right where he wanted me. Surrendering to him,

I closed my eyes and rested my cheek against the marble. I let the wickedness of his tongue overwhelm me until I was rising up on tiptoes and straining against the wave of an impending orgasm.

"Ben!" I came with a shout. Panting and slapping at the countertop, I tried to escape his tongue but he was so strong. I gasped when he suddenly spun me around and lifted my legs until they were on his shoulders. I fell back onto my palms and arched my back as his sinful mouth found my clit. I grabbed the back of his head, threading my fingers through his thick hair and taking hold.

At first, I wanted to pull him away, to beg for mercy, but then his tongue flicked in a way that made my legs shake. I decided it was better to hold him right there, right where I needed him most. When my second climax hit, I let go completely. Head tipped back, I closed my eyes and rode the waves of explosive bliss.

With gentle kisses on my lower belly and inner thighs, Ben brought me down from that orgasmic high. He stood and grabbed the closest hand towel to wipe his shiny mouth and chin. He looked utterly debauched, eyes dark with lust and skin flushed with exertion.

Aching for him, I slid off the counter and grabbed the waistband of his shorts. In a few seconds, he was completely naked. I clasped his thick, hard cock and stroked it slowly, my grip loose and easy. Ben deftly unwound my now messy bun and tossed aside the hair tie. He combed his fingers through my hair until he had a handful of it at the base of my head.

With a shift of his hips, he pressed his cock against my waiting, willing mouth. He was the first partner I had ever trusted to take total control when I was on my knees. He liked to push my boundaries, but he respected the hard limits. It was a give and take that worked for us.

"Suck," he ordered in that low growl that made my pussy clench.

I traced his shaft with my tongue and then swallowed as much of his length as I could handle. He groaned and pumped his hips, sliding his cock in a little deeper before pulling back completely. Holding his fiery gaze, I smiled around his dick and sucked him right back into my mouth. He swore softly and let me have my way with him, bobbing and stroking until he was shaking and right on the edge.

Sensing he wasn't sure whether to let go, I looked up at him and begged for his cum. "Come in my mouth, Ben."

"Christ, Aston," he growled and slipped his shaft between my lips again. A few more strokes of my mouth, and he damn near roared as he came. I grasped his taut ass, my fingernails digging into his hot skin, and swallowed him as deep as I could. He shuddered against me, and I sat back on my heels, swallowing and grinning up at him. He ran his thumb over my lips and said, "You dirty, beautiful girl."

He helped me to my feet and drew me into his embrace. His hand swept up and down my back before tenderly patting my bottom. "You ready for bed, baby?"

I had planned to do some late-night reading for work, but I could already feel my eyelids drifting closed. "Yes."

"Come here," he said a little while later, gathering me in as I climbed into bed after tidying up and finding a nightgown.

Tucked against him, I closed my eyes and listened to the soothing thud of his heartbeat under my ear. Drowsy, I traced one of the outlines of his tattoos. He smoothed a hand down my hair and asked, "What did you want to tell me earlier?"

My fingertip faltered on the dark line of an eagle's feather on his chest. "A detective came to see me this morning."

Ben's hand stilled on the back of my head. "What did he want?"

"To talk about Calvin."

He stiffened under me. "What did he want to know about that piece of shit?"

"He's trying to track him down for questioning. He said that Calvin's associates had gone missing. He seems to think Calvin had another scam going. Something to do with real estate and maybe the husband of one of my coworkers." I swallowed nervously. "Do you think the detective knows what really happened to Calvin?"

"No. Even if Calvin had told someone he was coming back to this house or even if his phone was tracked here, it left with him. He visited. He left. You don't know what happened after that."

"I was vague about the last time I saw him. I said it had been a few weeks."

"That's good. It gives you cover if he comes back with more questions."

"Do you think he'll come back?"

"Yes." He brushed a tender kiss to my forehead. "We haven't seen the last of the police. Do you have a lawyer?"

"I have several on retainer. One of them is a defense attorney. Should I call him?"

"No. Let it ride for now. Act like you have nothing to hide."

That was easier said than done.

CHAPTER SIX

"SORRY!" MARLEY APOLOGIZED as she practically flew into the restaurant where we were meeting for brunch. Unsurprisingly, we looked as if we had coordinated our outfits. We both had chosen black leggings, oversized sweaters with lacy bralettes underneath and ballet flats. I'd chosen a pale green sweater and dark green bralette while she had gone with a peach sweater and black lace. "I'm so late! Did we miss our reservation?"

"Calm down," I urged, hugging her quickly. "They're running behind. We don't have a table yet." Noticing how harried she looked, I gave her long, loose braid a tug. "What's wrong?"

She rolled her eyes and sighed. "My mom."

"Uh-oh."

"McNeil? Party of two?" the hostess called.

Marley followed me to the hostess station and then across the restaurant to our cozy table by a window. We both ordered drinks—a Bloody Mary for me and a lemonade mimosa for her—and waited until our waiter was gone to talk.

"So…your mom?"

"I don't even know what to do with her anymore." Marley silenced her phone before dropping it into her purse. "I went to the pharmacy last night and picked up her prescriptions so I stopped by the house to drop them off. First of all, she has a new doctor—and I use the term 'doctor' lightly here because I'm pretty this guy is a fucking quack. The list of drugs he has her on is insane. That doesn't even include the shit she's taking without a prescription. I told her she's going to die if she keeps taking this crap, but she won't listen. I even offered to buy good weed off of Nate Reyes if she would give up the pain and sleep meds. She wouldn't even think about it."

"Jesus," I whispered.

"Then, there were, like, thirteen packages on the front porch. Half of them were from QVC and that damn jewelry channel she won't stop watching. There was a stack of mail on the kitchen table at least this high." She held her hand up to show me. "It was all past due bills and letters from the bank and IRS. I had to whip out my phone and pay her utilities right then and there so she'd have electricity and water. The mortgage is behind, and I don't have enough in savings to cover it."

"I thought your mom's house was paid off."

"It is." Marley frowned. "Was."

"She took out a second mortgage?"

"From the looks of it, yep."

"How far behind is she?"

"Three."

I winced. "She's close to foreclosure."

"That's what I got from her stack of nastygrams from the bank." Marley considered the menu in front of her for a moment. "What are you getting?"

"I'm so hungry," I said, turning my attention to the menu. "My stomach was weird this morning before I hit the gym so I had some coffee and that's it."

"You getting sick?"

I shrugged. "Maybe."

She leaned forward and asked, "Are you pregnant?"

"No!"

"Are you sure?"

I rolled my eyes. "I had my period, like, two weeks ago."

It had been a few days late and lighter than usual, but I had chalked it up to the nightmare I had survived. My body had always been sensitive to stress. Exams, track meets, debates—they all affected my cycle.

"It's probably just stress," I decided. "I always get sick to my stomach when I feel pressured or anxious."

"Work?" she guessed.

"Family," I said, giving her a pointed look.

Her eyes widened. "Oh no."

"Yeah." Looking at the menu, I said, "I sort of want the huevos rancheros but also a burger. And some queso and guacamole," I added, noticing the appetizer section. "And maybe some fried green tomatoes."

"Let's order it all," Marley decided, putting down her menu. "Between the two of us, we can demolish that easy."

She was right, of course. On more than one occasion, Ben had been stunned by the amount of food the two of us could put away. "I'm game."

When our waiter returned with our drinks, he raised an eyebrow at our order, especially when Marley added shrimp and grits. "I'll be right back with your appetizers. Do you need another drink?"

"Just iced tea," Marley answered.

"Same," I said, handing back my menu. After a quick sip of my Bloody Mary, I asked, "Does Spider know about your mom's money problems?"

"Probably." She played with the candied lemon slice on the rim of her glass. "They haven't stayed under the same roof for, what, seven years? He gives her money and space, and she seems happy with that." Her lips puckered from the tartness of her drink, and she placed it back on the table. "I don't know why they haven't divorced."

"Habit," I guessed. "Their relationship status must work for them."

"They're both miserable." She sighed and rubbed her face with both hands. "Mom is going to ruin us with her fucking shopping addiction and these stupid businesses she keeps joining."

In all the years I had known Marley, her mother had always struggled with money management. Her stepdad's position in the outlaw motorcycle club had always provided his family with a steady income. Marley never should have gone without, but her mother spent money on the craziest shit. I couldn't even count the number of times Marley had a negative lunch account or couldn't go on a field trip or had holes in her shoes.

When we were younger, I had always tried to help her, but she had explained that we couldn't be friends if I was always going to try to give her money. It made her feel unequal and indebted. She wanted to be my friend, not a charity case. It was hard enough for her being the little girl from the trailer park who had her tuition paid for by scholarships. I didn't like watching her struggle, but I had respected her wishes.

She had been out the door at eighteen, moving right out into a small mobile home in one of Spider's parks. Since then, she hadn't ever been without at least one job. There had been a stretch one summer where she had worked three jobs—the pawn shop, waitressing and stocking shelves overnight at Walmart. She seemed to always be saving and squirreling away money. She swore some day she was going to take a trip to Europe, but she always had an excuse for postponing and waiting.

"What business has she started this time?" I asked, certain it was some version of a pyramid scheme. In the last few years, she had sold leggings, jewelry, candles, essential oils and two different weight loss products. It was always some get-rich-quick scheme that left her broke and even more in debt.

"Makeup." She took a long drink. "That's what was in the rest of the boxes on the porch. She said she needed inventory for hosting parties."

"Oh, no."

"Yeah."

"Does she expect you to host one?"

"After she dragged me to that creepy sex toy party at her friend's house, she's never asked me to be any part of her wild MLM adventures."

I shuddered at the memory. Marley had marched into my house so angry that night. Her face had been almost tomato red as she had recounted sitting in a living room crammed with her mom's friends while a consultant waved around dildos and vibrators and talked about all the bizarre uses for the company's patented shaving lotion. She wasn't a prude by any stretch of the imagination, but being pressured into buying a sex toy and asked super invasive questions by a stranger had humiliated her.

The waiter returned with our starters and teas. After he left, Marley grabbed a chip and dragged it through the mound of bright green guacamole. I sensed she needed a break from thinking about her mom. "So, Ben joined me for dinner with Nina and Pedro."

"How did that go?" Marley seemed hesitant to even ask.

"Surprisingly well," I admitted. "Mostly."

"Mostly?"

"She interrogated him about his religion and gave me a guilt trip about missing Mass."

"Uh-oh."

"Super awkward for a bit," I said, snatching another chip from the basket. "Other than that, it was okay. Except for the part where Ben was late and showed up covered in dried blood," I added before drowning my chip in queso.

"What?"

"Ben was at Phan's yesterday," I explained and grabbed a napkin.

"Are you serious? I saw it on the news last night. It looked really bad. Is he okay?"

"He's fine. It wasn't his blood."

"Thank goodness!" She turned pensive as she sipped her mimosa. "You know what's strange?"

"What?"

"That truck that slammed into the noodle shop?"

"The red one?"

She nodded. "I think it was at the pawn shop on Thursday night."

"Think or know?"

"Think," she said, reaching for some more chips. "I was working the night shift, and a guy came in trying to pawn off jewelry, handbags, electronics…" She waved her hand. "High-end stuff. Like really good stuff."

"But?"

"There was something off about him. Like he had weird vibes," she explained. "He seemed nervous and was super sweaty. I decided not to buy anything from him. I wasn't sure if it was stolen or not."

"Was he the one driving the red truck?"

"He was cussing up a storm on his way out the door. I saw the red truck shoot out of the parking lot right after that. He must have been driving it."

Glancing around to make sure no one was actively listening to us, I leaned forward and lowered my voice. "Ben said the guys in the red truck robbed a stash house before the accident at Phan's. He thinks they were the same thieves who robbed two of their guys on Thursday night."

"Are you serious?"

"Deadly."

"Shit. I guess it's a good thing I didn't buy from that guy. The last thing the shop needs is the police digging through the inventory and closing us down for a few days."

"Do you think you should call the police and let them know you saw the truck?"

She made a face. "Probably."

I understood her reticence toward dealing with the police. It wasn't easy being Spider's stepdaughter. Knowing I had to add to her worries, I hesitantly said, "Listen, um, a detective came to see me yesterday."

"Because of something to do with Ben?" she guessed.

I shook my head. "Calvin."

Her eyes widened. "Why?"

"He's missing," I said, holding her gaze and hoping she would understand what I was trying to tell her without actually saying it. "The police want to ask him some questions."

"I see." She broke a chip into pieces. "Well, who knows where he is? It's not as if you guys are close."

"That's what I explained to the detective." My gaze drifted toward the approaching waiter. I waited until he had delivered our food and drinks and left to resume our sensitive conversation. "I told the detective I would contact him if I saw Calvin."

"That's all you can do," she said, reaching for her fork. "So, what are you wearing to the wedding?"

Once we started talking about dresses and shoes and jewelry, our brunch date became much more relaxed, exactly what we needed. Now that we were both in grad school, we seemed to have less and less time to spend together like this. By the time we finished dessert, we were both flushed from laughing.

"What are your plans for tonight?" I asked while scribbling a tip amount on the receipt.

"I'll probably stay home and read," she said, checking her phone. A second later, she confessed, "CJ asked me out again."

Excited, I dropped the pen. "And?"

She shrugged. "I don't know. I wasn't really feeling second date vibes with him."

I rolled my eyes and huffed. "You say that about everyone you date."

"Which makes me think I'm meeting the wrong guys," she

countered. "I liked CJ. Our date was great, and he was a lot of fun. I just couldn't see anything developing between us. He travels all the time and has a demanding schedule."

"He's a freaking basketball player," I interjected. "Like a legit professional NBA player. Sure, his schedule is rough, but he's got a real future ahead of him."

"Maybe that's not the future I want," she replied with a shrug.

"What do you want?" I asked seriously. "What would make you happy?"

She thought about it and finally said, "Stability. Someone who is going to be there when I wake up and when I go to bed. Someone who is done with all the partying and drinking and smoking."

"So…like an old guy?" I teased.

She frowned at me. "Not *that* old. Just, you know, settled."

I didn't want to point out that she was describing the opposite of her stepdad. She loved Spider and would defend him to anyone who ever had a bad thing to say, but it was clear that he hadn't provided the most stable home life. Her mother didn't help matters any. It was no wonder she wanted a relationship with someone who could give her what she had craved the most as a child.

Another thought struck me. A bit slyly, I asked, "What about a certain slightly older guy who took an actual bullet for you?"

She blushed so hard the tips of her ears turned pink. "He's not interested in me like that."

"Are you kidding me?" My jaw dropped. "He's totally into you."

She shook her head. "If he was into me, he would have made a move by now."

"Maybe he thinks you aren't into him?"

"Maybe."

"Well, why don't you shoot your shot?"

She wrinkled her nose. "I think he might be offended if I asked him out for a drink. He's kind of, well, you know, old school alpha about things."

"I could tell Ben to tell him that you're interested."

She laughed. "Are we in eighth grade again?"

"I'm just trying to help!"

"I know you are." She reached across the table and touched my hand. "Let it go. If it's meant to be, it will happen."

I didn't want to let it go. I wanted to play matchmaker, but I had to respect her wishes, even if it frustrated me.

After leaving the restaurant, I cut across town to Allure and made it through the door with barely five minutes until the start of my mani-pedi and blowout appointment. Once I was checked in, I hurried to the ladies room so I wouldn't be squirming in my chair later or penguin waddling to the bathroom with wedges between my freshly painted toes.

I had just closed my stall door when another client came into the bathroom. She was hissing angrily into her phone and seemed upset as she closed herself in the stall at far end of the row. I tried not to eavesdrop, but the echo of the tiled room made it impossible to ignore.

"How?" she asked furiously. "How the *fuck* do escrow funds disappear?"

My eyes widened as I tried to handle my business as quietly as possible. Someone had stolen her escrow funds?

"No, you listen, Gary," she snarled, "I don't want to hear any more of your bullshit excuses! I want my client's money by nine a.m. on Monday or else I'm calling the police, the FBI, the FDIC, the IRS and the reporter at the Chronicle who handles finance stories. You get that money—or else I will destroy you. And your wife," she added meanly.

The angry woman wrenched open her stall door and stormed out of the bathroom, leaving me wondering what the hell I had just overheard. As I stood at the sink washing my hands, a suspicion began to take hold. The detective had shown me a photo of Gary Metcalf. Betty had mentioned Margie leaving in tears after a visit from a federal agent. Were those two things connected to the phone call I had just heard?

I waited until my feet were soaking in a pool of warm, bubbling water to pick up my phone. It didn't take me long to find Gary Metcalf and his company. After a little more Googling, I learned about the IRS regulations on real estate sales and postponing or avoiding capital gains taxes. The IRS allowed investment property owners to deposit their profits from the sale of one property with an intermediary like Gary to avoid paying capital gains. He held the money in escrow, profiting off the interest and fees.

Was he embezzling from his clients? Was that why Margie had been visited by a federal agent? Did she know that he was misusing client funds?

And how did Calvin fit into all of this? Had he sold some of the properties he had inherited and put his money with Gary? Knowing Calvin, he had likely figured out some way to work the system and make money off of the 1031 exchanges. Had he owed money to Gary? Or did Gary owe him?

Those thoughts plagued me as I tried to enjoy the rest of my appointment. Normally, the salon was my happy place. I enjoyed being pampered. I lived for lazy Saturdays like this.

But there was nothing happy about the thoughts swirling around in my head. I felt as if I were trapped in the center of a tangled web that Calvin had woven, and the police, like a horde of venomous spiders, were about to get me.

CHAPTER SEVEN

"After the ceremony, you'll make your way to the reception. There will be a cocktail hour, probably some champagne and light canapes," Alina explained while pouring tea in the opulent solarium of her grand home. "Milk?"

Ben nodded and waited to take the cup from her. "Are there rules about how much to eat or drink?"

"I usually have two or three canapés and one cocktail or flute of champagne." She dropped a single cube of sugar in her cup. "You'll likely be very busy meeting people and shaking hands. Keep that in mind."

"Right." He plucked two sugar cubes from the jar and plopped them into his cup. The dainty spoon felt ridiculous in his hands, but he remembered not to clank it against the sides of the cup as he stirred gently. "And after the cocktail hour?"

"You'll find your seating cards and make your way into the dining area. Make sure to pull out Aston's chair," she said pointedly. "You're a gentleman. Remember that."

"I will," he promised. Having grown up inside Alina's manor, he had learned most of the rules of etiquette at an early age. He might have been raised in an infamous and exclusive whore house, but he has been taught to be respectable and decent.

"I had Joachim set the table for you. When you're done with tea, we'll sit in the dining room and refresh your memory." Sitting back in her plush chair, she crossed her legs and sipped her tea. Like a queen holding court, she smiled indulgently at him. "Now, tell me how things are going with Aston."

"Good." He snatched one of the annoyingly small sandwiches from the tiered tray. It was delicious, but he felt like a clumsy giant trying to eat it.

"Just good?" Her mischievous expression warned him that she would needle him until she got the information she wanted. "I've heard that you've been spending most nights with her."

Aggravated, he said, "Besian gossips more than an old woman."

"I didn't hear it from him."

Reaching for another of the salmon sandwiches, Ben narrowed his eyes. "Are you having me followed?"

"Now, why would I do that?"

"Because you promised my mother you would look after me," he replied before drinking his tea.

"I'm not having you followed." She set aside her cup and saucer. "I have a client who lives next door to Aston. He hears your motorcycle. He's worried Aston is bringing a criminal element into the neighborhood."

Ben chortled. "He complains about the criminal element while being entertained by a million-dollar madam?"

"You know how those federal judges can be."

"Hypocritical?"

"Something like that." Her coy smile faded as her expression turned serious. "Ben, are you going to ask me?"

"Ask you what?"

She sighed and leaned back in her chair. "About Aston's father."

Ben grimaced as the question he had been steadfastly ignoring was thrust in front of him. "I'm not sure I want to ask that."

"Because you'll have to tell Aston?"

"Because I'll have to hide it from her," Ben countered. "She doesn't need to know about her father's habits, and he deserves to keep his secrets, even if he's dead."

"It wasn't like that with him, Ben. He wasn't here to sate any sort of strange appetites. He was just lonely. He was a rich, lonely man who wanted someone to love him without the work of romance or the risk of heartbreak."

He was glad to hear that Aston's father hadn't come to Alina seeking one of the girls who catered to bizarre fetishes. He didn't care what people did behind closed doors, but it would have been a difficult secret to keep.

"Did you know when you met her?"

"Know what?" he asked, confused.

"That you had seen her father here," she clarified.

He shook his head. "I didn't recognize him until I saw a picture of him at her house. He had seemed familiar to me, but I had assumed I had seen him at a poker game or one of the casinos. It was the tattoo," he explained, gesturing toward his chest. "That shield with the fish and two books."

"Dolphin," Alina corrected. "It's a dolphin between the books."

"If you say so," he replied. "In the picture, Aston and her

dad were on a yacht, and he didn't have a shirt. I saw the tattoo and remembered seeing him in the hallway that night that fat old fuck from L.A. had a heart attack with Brianna."

Alina pursed her lips at the mention of that night. "Yes, that was quite a commotion."

"Once I realized why he looked familiar, I decided it wasn't any of my business."

"You're right. It's not, but better that she should hear it from you than someone else who might want to hurt her with a nasty story."

He hadn't thought of it that way. "Shit."

"Just consider telling her," Alina suggested. "You know her best. You know what she can handle and what she can't. And it's Wharton," she added as an afterthought.

Thrown by her comment, Ben asked, "The fat fuck from L.A.? Was that his name?"

She rolled her eyes and laughed. "No, Ben. The tattoo. It's the Wharton shield. It's a very prestigious business school."

"Of course, it is," he grumbled. Wanting to change the subject, he asked, "How have you been? Any trouble I need to sort out?"

"Business is steady. Clients are well-behaved." She dismissively waved her hand. "I'm more worried about you. What was that mess at Phan's?"

"Bullshit," he said, reaching for the teapot to refill his cup. It wasn't the correct way of doing things, and Alina arched an eyebrow but didn't stop him. "The same jackass that robbed us decided to rob a stash house for cash and product. There was a chase and a shootout. The driver managed to survive and escape."

"And the bosses?"

"Had a long meeting last night," he said, pouring milk into his cup. "I had to hear all about it this morning."

"And?"

He shrugged and stirred his tea until the sugar cubes dissolved. "Lots of talking. No action."

"Well, they can't hit back blindly," she reasoned.

Skipping the scones, he chose one of the chocolate pastries. "I don't think it's any of the usual suspects. It feels like a lucky amateur."

"Any leads on the truck or driver?"

"The truck was reported stolen last year. The driver is in the wind. None of the guys at the stash house recognized him."

"And the second person in the truck? The one who died at the scene?"

"He was a nobody." Ben took another pastry from the tray. "Kostya passed around his face and name this morning. No one recognized him. He ran a small import shop."

"That's all very odd," she remarked and leaned forward to select a cucumber sandwich. Sitting back, she nibbled on it a bit. "Do you think it's someone who owes money to one of the bosses? A gambling debt? A drug debt?"

"Maybe."

"Hopefully, it will end with the mess at Phan's."

"Hopefully."

After they finished their tea, Alina led him into the formal dining room. She gave him a quick tutorial on how to select the correct glass and when to use each fork. "If you get confused, just wait for Aston or someone else at the table to make a move. As long as you are kind and friendly, no one is going to care if you grab the wrong spoon."

"Friendly isn't really my thing," he groused, thinking of how ridiculous all of this was.

"I'm sure Aston would disagree." She fluffed the shaggy ends of his hair and smiled warmly. "She must care very deeply for you."

"She does," he agreed, feeling a tight squeeze in his chest. She loved him, even with his faults and criminal connections. The least he could do was make her proud tonight. Reaching up to touch his hair, he said, "I'm getting it cut after I leave here."

"Good." Alina seemed pleased. "You're so handsome when your hair is shorter."

"Okay, Mom," he replied sarcastically.

She narrowed her eyes and thumped him on the neck. "Brat."

They were both laughing when Big John, her daytime bouncer-slash-butler came into the dining room. "Madam Alina, your lawyer is here."

Ben frowned. "On a Saturday? Christ, what's the hourly rate for that!"

"Exorbitant," she replied with a wan smile. Turning to Big John, she said, "Send him into my office, please."

After Big John left, Ben asked, "Is it serious? What kind of charges?"

She shook her head. "It's not anything criminal. It's real estate."

"Real estate?"

Alina sighed. "I'm having some issues with an intermediary. It will all sort itself out in the end."

"If you need any help…"

"I'll let you know." She patted his chest. "Go get your haircut. Don't worry about tonight. You'll be fine."

He leaned in and pecked her cheek. "Thank you for tea."

"Next time, bring Aston."

Wondering how awkward that would be, he nodded. "Sure."

Out in the warm afternoon sun, he pulled on his helmet and kicked his bike to life. He roared down the beautifully manicured streets of the outrageously expensive old neighborhood. The ride to the barbershop was nice and gave him time to think about work, both legal and illegal. Business was good. He might even hit the goals for his five-year plan twelve to eighteen months early. That made all of the long hours and backbreaking labor worth it.

But the other business—the illegal shit—seemed to only get riskier and more dangerous. For a long time, he had enjoyed the thrill of illicit activities. There was something invigorating about breaking the law and getting away with it. It was wrong, but it felt good.

Until Aston.

Now, he had a clear vision of a future that didn't include boosting and chopping cars or running security for high stakes poker games and gambling dens. He could see the possibilities a life with Aston promised, and the thought of risking those possibilities made his stomach hurt. He just didn't know how to get out.

The thought plagued him as he sat for his haircut. The visit with Alina had spurred memories of his mother. Would she have been proud of him? She would have been proud of

the business he had built, but she would have been heartbro-
ken to learn he had chosen his father's family and the mafia
over a simple, quiet life as an upstanding citizen. She had
wanted so much more for him. She had wanted him to have a
good job, a nice girl and a family. That was all she wanted for
him.

By the time he left the barbershop, his mood had shifted to
one that was darker. He tried not to indulge the self-loathing
that came with the thoughts of disappointing his mother, but
it was hard to ignore them. When he finally reached Aston's
house, he felt jumpy and irritated and desperately needed to
burn off some energy. Remembering the lawn mower he had
promised to fix, he walked out to the landscaping shed and
worked to diagnose and fix the issue. It didn't take long to
repair the trimmer either.

Still feeling antsy, he searched for a new project. Spotting
Baby, the vintage car that had brought Aston into his life, he
knew what to do. A few hours later, he was buffing the final
coat of wax onto the sleek curves of the car when Aston's
garage door opened. She pulled into her usual spot, killing the
engine on her old but well-maintained Jeep, and got out with a
smile on her face. With black flats dangling from one hand,
she closed the distance between them in a pair of disposable
flip-flops. He frowned at the sight of them on her pampered
little feet. As if reading his mind, she said, "I drove really
carefully."

"Those things are dangerous as fuck, baby." He dropped
the microfiber towel he had been using on the hood of the car
and reached for her, dragging her into a lingering embrace.
"You're going to get those caught on the accelerator one of

these days."

Although he had expected her to argue, she kissed his cheek and said, "You'll just have to start taking me for my pedicures."

His lips twitched. "Hell, maybe I'll book one with you."

She laughed and pressed her lips to his in a playful kiss. "You might like being pampered."

"I might," he conceded and let her go.

"How is Alina?"

"She's good. I promised her I would bring you over for tea one afternoon."

"Really?" Her eyes damn near sparkled with interest. "I get to go back?"

"Only you would find a visit to a brothel that exciting."

"Because it is exciting," she insisted. "It's kind of naughty, you know? How often do I get to do naughty things?"

"You want to do something naughty right now?" He eyed the hood of the car, and she blushed prettily.

"Ben," she said his name in that disapproving way that always made him smile. Reaching out, she touched his hair. "I like this."

"Yeah?" He hadn't been so sure about the short length and fade, but if she was happy, he was, too. Picking up the towel, he decided to check for any dull spots. "How's Marley?"

"Lovesick."

"For the basketball player?" he asked, hoping that wasn't the case for Besian's sake.

"Nope." Aston smiled mischievously. "For your boss."

He straightened up from the spot he had been inspecting. "Are you serious?"

She nodded. "She thinks he's not interested."

Ben scoffed. "I caught him in a bookstore yesterday buying a stack of books about feminism."

"No!" Aston's jaw dropped.

"Yes. I even helped him pick one out," he admitted.

She looked even more amused now. "Which one?"

"The one about the room."

"Virginia Woolf? I'm impressed, Arben Beciraj."

Tucking the microfiber cloth into his back pocket, he reached for her again and dragged her close. He nuzzled her neck. "I've got something else that will impress you."

"Ben," she whispered heatedly. "We have to get ready for the wedding."

"I'll make it quick," he promised and captured her mouth in a rough, demanding kiss.

WITH A FRUSTRATED growl, Ben ripped the bow tie from his neck. He scowled at the damn thing in the reflection of the long mirror in the corner of Aston's room. Even after watching a YouTube video and reading a step-by-step tutorial, he couldn't figure it out.

"Need some help?" Aston walked into the bedroom while threading earrings through her pierced lobes. "I could hear you growling across the hall in Dad's room."

He waved the black strip of fabric. "Do I have to wear this?"

"Yes."

His gaze drifted to the slow swing of her hips as she crossed the room. *Fuck.* She looked amazing in her dark blue dress. It hugged her waist and skimmed her ass in a way that made him want to peel it off her as slowly as possible. After quickly bending her over the hood of the freshly waxed car, he now wanted to unwrap her like a gift and spend the whole night making her tremble and pant and beg for his cock.

"Stop looking at me like that," she scolded as she placed something on the nearby ottoman.

"Like what?" He put his hands on her hips and drew her in closer.

"Like you want to use this to tie me to the headboard," she said, taking the tie from him.

"Not a bad idea," he murmured as he peppered kisses down the side of her neck.

"Later," she said and kissed his cheek. "I could barely get this damn thing zipped. I'm not going through that again. Now—straighten up."

He did as she instructed but kept his hands on her hips. She smelled so good. It was a different scent than she normally wore, darker and spicier. Her lips were redder than usual, and her eye makeup sexier and bolder. He wanted to kiss her. Hard.

"It's smudge-proof," she said as if reading his mind.

"You want to test it out?"

"Let me finish this first." Her hands moved skillfully, looping and tugging and tightening. She took a little step back to examine her work and then stepped forward again to adjust the knot. "Okay. What do you think?"

Reluctant to let go of her, he turned to study his reflection. "It looks great."

"You look great," she praised as he turned back to face her.

She brushed her hands over his shoulders, and the light glinted off the diamonds in her gold bracelet and cocktail ring. The look on her face softened. "My dad taught me how to do that. He said someday I might have a husband or sons who would need my help."

Seeing the flash of grief in her eyes, he cupped her face and kissed her tenderly. "I'm sorry your father isn't here tonight."

"It's okay," she whispered, sliding into his embrace. "I have you."

Careful not to disturb her hair, he rubbed her back and kissed her cheek. "Do you think he would have liked me?"

"After seeing the way you hand washed and detailed Baby for tonight?" She leaned back and smiled up at him. "He would have given me the talk about not letting you go."

"My mother would have loved you," Ben asserted. "When I was getting my hair cut earlier, I kept thinking about how my mom would have been so happy to us together like this. She would have been thrilled to see me in a suit with my hair cut and my shoes shined."

"I wish I could have met her."

"So do I," he murmured, allowing himself a moment of wistful pain.

"I have something I want you to wear tonight." She picked up something shiny from the ottoman. "I gave these to my dad on his fiftieth birthday. I think they're perfect for you."

"Aston, I can't take your dad's cufflinks," he protested as she opened her palm to show him. "Those were special to him."

"They were, and they're special to me. I want you to wear them tonight."

With a nod, he relented. "If that's what you want."

"It is." She handed him one to inspect. "They're made from vintage car parts. These were from a '68 Corvette."

"Okay. That's cool as shit." He examined the square stamped cufflink. It had a nice patina and a little weight in his hand.

She laughed. "I figured you would like them."

"I do. Thank you for letting me borrow them."

"You're welcome." She took the cufflink from his hand and fastened it in place. "There."

He bent down to capture her mouth in an appreciative kiss. "We better get on the road."

"Let me grab my clutch."

While she disappeared into the bathroom and walk-in closet, he checked his phone. There were a few messages from Jet in coded language letting him know the security team was together for the poker game. He didn't think the guy who had robbed them would be stupid enough to try it again, but they had to be prepared.

"Ben, I forgot to tell you something that Marley mentioned at brunch," Aston said as she came back into the bedroom with a pale gold clutch in hand. With a teasing scowl, she added, "You distracted me."

"You enjoyed it," he countered, remembering how loud she had been toward the end.

"Not the point," she said, flicking his chest. "So, Marley and I were talking about the thing that happened at Phan's yesterday."

"And?"

"And she said that she thought she recognized the red

truck."

"Was she sure?"

"She seemed fairly certain it was the same truck that had been at the pawn shop the night before," Aston explained. "She said the guy was giving off weird vibes, and she decided to not buy from him or loan him any cash. She figured he was trying to fence stuff he stole."

"Do you think the security cameras might have gotten his face?" he asked, already reaching for his phone.

"I think there's a good chance." Then with a sly little smile, she suggested, "You should have your boss drop by the shop to ask her."

Ben leveled a look at her. "I see what you did there."

"What?" she feigned innocence.

"You really want to play matchmaker with those two?"

She shrugged. "If it's meant to be, it will happen."

Even though he wasn't sure it was a good idea for Marley and Besian to get together, he nevertheless sent a message to the boss. As he trailed Aston downstairs and out into the garage, he imagined how messy a love affair between an Albanian mob boss and the daughter of an outlaw MC's president could get. If things went south, sides would have to be taken. It would not end well for anyone.

Then again, if things went well…

"What are you doing?" Ben asked as Aston made her way to the driver's side.

"Driving us to the wedding," she said matter-of-factly.

"In those heels?" They were at least three inches, sharp and thin. He didn't even know how she could balance in them, especially considering there were only slim golden strips wrapping around her ankles.

"What's wrong with them?"

"Nothing," he said, enjoying the way they made her legs look, "if you're walking or dancing, but driving?" He shook his head and flicked his fingers for the keys. "No way."

She pouted but handed over the keys anyway. "Fine."

He snatched her hand before she could move away and tugged her in close. With his other hand, he outlined the curve of her perfect ass and the smooth plane of her thigh before sliding under her dress to cup her bare cheek. "Let me drive now. I'll let you drive later."

His meaning wasn't lost on her. With a grin, she kissed him. "Deal."

CHAPTER EIGHT

W HILE I WAITED for Ben to handle the valet, I smiled at the few wedding guests I recognized milling around the entrance to the venue. Ben threaded his arm through mine, and I let him take the lead, guiding me into the beautifully decorated foyer. Although this was Oliver's fourth wedding, he had clearly spared no expense. I lingered near one of the flower arrangements outside the ceremony space to enjoy the pretty magnolias for a moment.

"If this is what his fourth wedding looks like, how crazy was the first one?" Ben asked in a whisper before taking two program cards from the basket.

"I don't remember the first one." I smiled at the usher who led us down the aisle. "I was only three or four."

We walked all the way down a row of empty seats on the groom's side and settled into our places. The chairs around us were starting to fill up and more than once I stood to hug and cheek kiss longtime family friends. Ben seemed not to mind being introduced over and over and shaking hands with strangers. I shot him an apologetic smile when we finally managed to sit down again.

With a shake of his head, Ben silently communicated that it wasn't a problem. He clasped my hand and interlaced our fingers before lifting my hand for a sweet kiss. He let me tug his hand into my lap, holding tight as the music shifted and the lights dimmed a bit. At the front of the elegantly decorated room, Oliver and his best man walked to the makeshift altar with the officiant. He seemed to be searching the room for someone, and when our gazes met, I realized it was me. He smiled at me, but I could see the sadness in his dark eyes at not having my dad standing next to him for the fourth time. I nodded slightly, letting him know I understood and shared his feelings.

The ceremony began with the most adorable little flower girls and a ring bearer. Bridesmaids and groomsmen followed, many of the groomsmen friends of my father's as well. When the bridal music began, we all stood to watch the procession of the bride and her father. I had met Lily back when my father had still been alive, only a few months before his metastasized cancer had finally taken him. She seemed lovely, very kind and obviously in love with Oliver. Maybe the fourth time would be the charm for him. Maybe Lily finally was The One.

When we sat, I noticed Ben looking at Lily with an odd expression, almost as if he recognized her. *Curious*, I thought, wondering where they had crossed paths. I held onto that question until the short ceremony ended. Tucked in tight to Ben's side, I followed the trail of guests leaving the ceremony space for the adjacent cocktail reception. I waited until we were out of the crush of people to ask, "Do you know her?"

"The bride?" He glanced down at me and nodded. "Not well, but I recognize her." He looked suddenly uncomfortable. "It might be strange for her to see me here."

"Why?"

He gently pulled me toward a more private area. Dipping down, he cupped my face and brushed his lips across my cheek. His mouth moved closer to my ear, and he whispered, "She was one of Alina's girls."

I schooled my features, not letting on that he had just dropped a bomb right in the middle of a wedding reception. To anyone else, we looked like two young lovers sharing a tender moment. I wanted to keep it that way.

"Aston?" He seemed worried now, his brow creased with concern.

"That can stay our secret."

"Of course," he agreed. "I wouldn't dare expose anyone like that." He hesitated. "Does it bother you?"

I frowned up at him. "Why in the world would that bother me? They're both adults." With a little shake of my head, I sent a pointed glance to the crowd surrounding us. "They're the ones who might make it a big deal."

His sharp gaze moved around the room. Eventually, he said, "There are enough of Alina's clients in here to make that unlikely. I don't think anyone will let on that they recognize each other."

Surprised by Ben's remark, I cast a surreptitious look around the room filled with Oliver and Lily's friends and family and wondered which of them were known clients. Another thought struck me, this one unwanted and uncomfortable. *What if my father...?*

"Aston!"

At the sound of that familiar, booming voice, I winced and waited for the inevitable awkwardness that was about to descend on us. Tad Gaines, one of the hottest players in professional football, strode toward me with that silly, boyish grin that used to make my stomach do somersaults. He swept me up in a bear hug that damn near crushed my lungs. I couldn't help but laugh at his enthusiasm. He'd always been a sweetheart of a man and kind to a fault.

"I told Britt that was you!" Tad set me back down. "You look great. How have you been?"

"Good." Glancing at Ben, I noticed his tight expression and hurriedly introduced him. "Tad, this is my boyfriend. Ben, this is my friend, Tad."

"Happy to meet you, Ben."

"Same," Ben said as he gripped Tad's hand. "That was a hell of a catch last game."

"It was lucky as heck," Tad replied with a laugh.

As they shook hands, both men seemed to be sizing up the other. They were similar in height and build, but different in every other way. Ben had dark hair where Tad was blond. Ben was quieter, more serious and brooding while Tad had a brash personality and enjoyed being the life of the party.

"Aston!" Brittany, Tad's heavily pregnant wife, joined us. Her gorgeous red hair fell in loose waves down her back, spurring envious thoughts as I imagined having been blessed with her hair genes. She had chosen a dress similar to mine in color, the dark blue contrasting beautifully against her hair.

"Britt!" I hugged her tightly. "It's so good to see you again."

"It's been a while," she said, her gaze softening as she rubbed my shoulder. "How have you been?"

"Good." I hadn't seen either of them since my father's funeral so her concern was touching. "It gets a little easier every day." I reached for Ben's hand and smiled up at him. "It helps to have someone like Ben in my corner."

His earlier unease vanished, and his expression turned tender and warm. His hand left hand drifted to the small of my back while the other reached out toward Brittany. "Ben Beciraj."

"Nice to meet you, Ben." She shot me a saucy look and raised her eyebrows as if impressed with him. "Do you two work together?"

"No, I own an auto shop."

"He helped me with my dad's favorite car," I added, sharing a secret smile with Ben. That was a very, very tame description of our first interaction.

"How about that!" Tad grinned and looked utterly pleased with himself. "Didn't I tell you that you'd find your perfect man in a garage?"

"You did," I agreed, remembering that conversation well. "When you retire from playing football, you should open a matchmaking service."

"Hell!" Tad laughed. "I just might." He slipped an arm around Brittany's shoulders and asked, "What do you think, darlin'?"

"Whatever you want, sweetheart." She patted his chest and then let her hand drift to the curve of her belly, the outrageously large diamond in her ring sparkling like a star.

"How are you feeling?" I asked, my gaze following her movement.

"Like a whale," Brittany replied with a laugh. "Seven more weeks until it's showtime."

"Fingers crossed it's not on a game day." Tad was teasing,

but I sensed he was actually worried about it. I couldn't even imagine what it would be like to miss his baby's birth, but I suspected his contract with the team would penalize him for missing a game.

"Did you get your baby shower invitation?" Brittany asked after playfully thumping her husband's arm.

"I did. I've already sent my RSVP to your sister." I didn't mention that I had spent almost two hours scouring her baby registry trying to decide what to buy while feeling woefully out of my depth.

Even though we wanted to chat more, Tad was pulled away to speak with another couple and Brittany dutifully followed. Alone with Ben, I decided to be proactive about the whole thing. "So, uh, we dated for a while."

"I figured," Ben said, reaching out to grab two flutes of champagne from a passing waiter. "How long?"

"Two years in high school and one year of college. Long distance," I added, taking a glass from him. "He was at Alabama, and I was here at Rice." Worried he might feel blindsided by meeting an old boyfriend of mine, I said, "I should have warned you he might be here. Oliver is his uncle. That's how we met when we were kids."

Ben frowned. "Aston, you don't have to justify your dating history to me."

"I know, but I'm sure I wouldn't be happy to see one of your old girlfriends picking you up and bear hugging you like that."

"I've never dated a girl that tall or strong," he replied, his mouth twitching with a hint of a smile.

A snort of laughter escaped me. "You know what I mean."

His big, warm hand settled against my face, and his thumb rubbed along the apple of my cheek. I leaned into his touch and closed my eyes for a moment, just enjoying the sensation of his heated skin on mine. It was a gesture that told me all I needed to know.

When I finally took a sip of my champagne, I grimaced. "Ugh."

"What's wrong?" Ben asked with concern.

"Tastes funny," I said, setting my glass on the tray of a passing waiter.

Ben took a tentative sip of his. "Tastes fine to me."

"Really?"

"Yeah." He glanced around and asked, "Do you want me to grab a pink cocktail from one of the waiters? No idea what's in it, but it looks like something you'd enjoy."

"No, I'll just stick to the punch."

Ben walked with me to the refreshment station so I could get a small cup of the cranberry red punch being served for the kids and teetotalers at the reception. Crisp and cold, it tasted delicious and was exactly what I needed. Side by side, we snatched a few canapes before finding ourselves pulled into a conversation with some of my coworkers. Despite Ben's distaste for social situations like these, he played the part well.

Betty, especially, seemed to adore him. "Sugar, you're even cuter in person. The first time you stop by the office, I'm stealing you away."

"I'd probably let you," Ben teased, taking her outrageous flirting in stride.

All around us, guests were starting to move toward the dining room. We joined the flow and waited to find our place cards.

"Lucky me," Betty announced as she found her place card put us at the same table. With a flirtatious grin, she slipped her arm around Ben's so he could escort us both into the dinner. "All right, handsome, lead the way."

She continued making moon eyes at Ben as dinner was served and the speeches began. Glad to see Ben relaxed and enjoying himself, I picked at the successive courses that appeared before me. My appetite had been off the last few days.

"Do you want to trade?" Ben had leaned over, his voice tinged with concern as he motioned toward my plate of filet mignon and roasted vegetables.

"No, but thank you for offering," I said, glancing at the lamb in front of him. "I'm fine."

"Are you sure?"

I reached under the table and patted his leg. "I'm sure. I'm saving room for cake."

He clearly wasn't convinced with my excuse but acquiesced with a nod. I managed to enjoy the sweet potatoes and parsnips and two bites of the flavorful filet before deciding I was done.

"Do you think Margie will be back at work on Monday?" Jed asked from his place across the table. He was addressing all of us, but only Betty answered.

"Not if Carrie was telling the truth," Betty said in that conspiratorial, gossipy tone that warned she had a juicy bit of news to tell.

"Carrie?" I asked, not recognizing the name as a fellow employee.

"She's at PwC," Jed explained and gestured to a table not far away. "She used to handle our outside auditing before she got promoted."

"She lives next door to Margie," Betty interjected. "When we were having cocktails earlier, she asked if I had spoken to Margie today."

"Why?" I held my breath, fearing the worst for Margie.

"Because, apparently," Betty drew out the word, "Margie's house was crawling with the Feds this morning."

"Oh, no," I gasped. "I really hope that's not true."

"So do I." Jed shook his head as he reached for his wine glass. "We'll have to let her go if it is."

"Why?" I couldn't think of a single reason to fire her. "She's great at her job. Our clients love her."

"If her husband is up to shady business, we can't have her in the office anymore," Jed insisted. "There's too much risk to our reputation."

"But...she has a new baby," I persisted. "We don't even know why there were agents at her place or what her husband did or didn't do. Even if he did do something illegal, she shouldn't be held responsible for that."

Jed smiled sadly. "You're young, kiddo. You haven't seen how ugly this business can get, how cutthroat we have to be sometimes. If Gary really did embezzle from his clients like everyone is saying, Margie is gone."

I wasn't so sure about that. I might not have an office in the C-suites yet, but the business was mine. My father had left it to me, with a few strings attached until I was ready to take over, but I wasn't going to let Jed or Oliver fire Margie if she had been blindsided by her husband's crimes.

"Who are Gary and Margie?" Ben asked as Oliver and Lily made their way to their cake.

"Margie is a risk analyst. Dad hired her right out of college, like, eleven or twelve years ago," I said, my voice soft as we moved our heads close together for some privacy. "Her husband is in trouble. He works in real estate."

"Like a realtor?"

"No. He handles financial arrangements. Well, he's supposed to handle them. He seems to have been stealing the money instead."

His expression turned pensive, as if he had just heard something interesting or important. I wanted to press him, to find out what he was thinking or knew, but the couple had just cut the cake and were feeding each other a piece. It was a sweet moment, and I happily clapped for them.

"Thank goodness!" Betty exclaimed as her slice of cake was placed in front of her. "Not a scrap of fondant to be seen. I'm so tired of having to peel away that powdered sugar Play-Doh." She cut into her cake with her dessert fork. "I blame Martha Stewart for making those abominations popular."

Ben shot me an amused look, and I couldn't help but laugh. It seemed Betty wasn't the only one who had enjoyed the cocktails and wine a little too much. The noise in the room started to rise as the guests loosened up and became more animated. Some of the men started slipping out of their tuxedo jackets or removing their bow ties altogether.

When the first dance started, Ben draped his arm over the back of my chair and gently clasped my shoulder. He kissed my temple, and I leaned into him. The familiar woodsy scent of his cologne surrounded me, and I wanted to snuggle in closer and place ticklish kisses along his jaw and neck until he broke and pinned me down for payback. We shared a private glance, one that made it clear that we both wanted to leave early.

So we did. After three dances, we made our exit, bypassing the crowd of guests still waiting to congratulate Oliver and Lily on our way out of the reception.

"I'm pretty sure we're breaking one of Alina's rules running out of here without talking to the bride and groom." Ben held my hand as we walked toward the front of the venue.

"We are," I agreed. "We'll have to apologize for being so rude with some flowers and a dinner invite."

"To a restaurant, I hope. Because if you cook dinner, we'll have to apologize again and send an even bigger flower arrangement."

"Jerk!" I swatted his chest even as I laughed. He wasn't wrong. My cooking skills were terrible. Poor Nina had tried for years to teach me the basics, but she had finally given up after choking on a bite of crunchy eggs seasoned with a few errant shards of eggshells.

"Mr. Beciraj!"

We both stopped at the sound of someone calling out for him. Ben let go of my hand and slid his arm around my waist, drawing me in close to his side in a protective manner. We turned to see Dr. Chowdhury, a highly sought-after dermatologist, striding toward us. I glanced up at Ben, wondering how the two had crossed paths.

"Aston," Dr. Chowdhury greeted with a stiff smile. It wasn't the easy grin he always had when he walked into the exam room to listen to my latest skin complaint. "Would you mind if I spoke to Ben for a moment?"

"Of course not." I stood nearby as Ben and Dr. Chow-dhury walked a short distance away for their conversation. Ben's body language had shifted from his earlier protective tenderness to the aggressive, cold stance that he had when dealing with business. From the looks of it, the doctor was in some kind of trouble. He had a pleading look on his face, and I tried not stare as Ben's hand sliced through the air in a gesture that seemed to end the conversation. Whatever Ben said to Dr. Chowdhury made the other man swallow nervously before pivoting on his heel and walking quickly back to the reception.

Ben gently took my arm and led me toward the doors. He clearly wanted to get the hell out of here. I bit back the endless questions I had as we waited for the valet to return with Baby, but as soon as I was buckled into my seat and Ben was next to me behind the wheel, I let loose.

"What was that about?"

"A debt."

"What kind of debt?"

"Gambling."

"Oh."

"Yeah."

"Like…how much?" I wondered as I toyed with the clasp of my clutch.

"Aston," he warned carefully.

"What? I'm just curious. I mean, he is my doctor and—"

"Not anymore," Ben interrupted with a stern look.

"What?"

"Dr. Chowdhury is not your doctor anymore. I don't want him touching you."

"Ben!" I frowned at him. "Don't be a possessive creep."

"Jesus, Aston," he said with a rough laugh. "That's not why I don't want him touching you."

"Oh. Well…why then?"

Ben tapped the side of his nose. "He doesn't just owe us money for bad bets. He's got a big fucking tab with his dealer across town. I don't want that coke addict anywhere near you."

I couldn't argue with that. Wondering if there were other doctors I should avoid, I asked, "Are there other doctors you wouldn't want me to see?"

He was quiet for a moment. "Yes."

"If I give you a list of the ones I see, can you check it?"

"Yes."

Another thought entered my mind. "Were there other people at the wedding you recognized? Other than Lily and the doctor?"

"There were."

"Like…a lot of them?"

"Yes."

"More than ten?"

He cracked a smile. "Yes."

"Twenty?"

"No."

"All of them gamblers or were some of them from Alina's?"

"Yes," he replied cryptically, the corners of his mouth lifting as he enjoyed teasing me with his non-answer.

The mention of Alina had me wondering about something else. My mind went back to the question that had developed after realizing that Oliver might have met Lily while she was a call girl. I wasn't sure I wanted the answer, but I had to ask anyway.

"Ben?"

"Yeah, baby?" He reached across the space between us to hold my hand.

"Did you ever see my dad at Alina's?"

His fingers flexed, and he waited a heartbeat too long to answer.

"Oh," I murmured. "Was he...? Did he go there a lot?"

"Aston." He sighed and seemed hesitant to continue. "Do you really want to know all of this?"

"I don't know," I admitted with a shrug. "Were you ever going to tell me?"

Ben glanced at me, his expression serious and dark. "No."

"Why not?"

"Because this is exactly how I worried this would go," he said, squeezing my hand. "Your dad was a good man. He loved you. He was a great father. But he was a man. He had needs. Men like your father—men with money and power—go to Alina because they trust her to be discreet. That discretion should continue after death."

Ben was right, of course. It wasn't my business where my father had sought out companionship. Still, it felt strange to think of my father going to a brothel or hiring a high-end escort. "Do you think he used Alina's services because he was too busy taking care of me to live the life he wanted?"

"No." Ben raised my hand and kissed it. "Don't even think like that."

"But why would he go to see a madam?"

"He probably wanted something simple and easy. No

strings attached," he added. "He was a busy man. He was used to delegating at work. It probably seemed natural to delegate finding dates to someone like Alina."

"I guess," I said uncertainly. "Maybe."

We lapsed into silence. It wasn't uncomfortable or tense. My mind was flooded with questions, and Ben seemed to understand that I needed some time to process my thoughts. In hindsight, I shouldn't have asked. I wasn't any happier knowing.

Sadness took hold as I thought of Dad sharing stolen nights here and there with call girls. Had his doomed and torturous marriage to my mother broken him? Had she soured him on love? Left him cold and unable to love another woman again?

After Ben parked and killed the engine, he unbuckled his seatbelt and turned to face me. He cupped the back of my neck and gently coaxed me to look at him. "I'm sorry that I upset you."

"You don't have to apologize for answering a question I asked." I leaned forward and touched my forehead to his. "I'm not upset."

"Are you sure?"

"I'm sure."

He didn't move. He simply waited, as if expecting me to say what was really bothering me. At first, I didn't want to voice it. I didn't want to go there. I didn't want to open up that chasm of grief and loss. It had been hard enough not to lose it earlier when I had ventured into Dad's room for those cuf-flinks.

"I miss my dad," I said finally. I tried to blink back the

tears in a futile attempt not to cry. "I miss my dad so much."

"I know you do, baby." He pulled me as close as he could and kissed my neck. "I wish there was some way to take away that pain, but you have to feel it. You have to accept it. You can't run from it."

I gripped the collar of his jacket and sobbed pitifully. It felt so painfully real sitting there in the front seat of my father's beloved car, coming straight from the wedding of his best friend. Adding in the new knowledge that my father had been so lonely that he had visited prostitutes made the grief almost unbearable. How had I been so blind to my father's sadness? To his emptiness? Why hadn't I been a better daughter?

"Let's go inside," Ben suggested gently. "Get out of these clothes and crawl into bed, huh?"

I couldn't think of anywhere else I wanted to be.

CHAPTER NINE

WAY TO GO, asshole.

Ben couldn't believe how badly he had fucked up their night. The vibe had been so good between them as they left the wedding. Before that jackass doctor had interrupted, he had been planning all the dirty things he wanted to do to Aston. The things that made her blush furiously and protest even as she encouraged him to keep going. The things that made her come so hard she would stop breathing and arch her back so sharply that he worried it would break.

Why the fuck didn't you lie?

It would have been so much easier to just lie to her about her father. Even after talking to Alina, he had been planning to keep that secret forever, but, in the moment, sitting that close to her, he hadn't been able to stomach the idea of lying to her. He didn't want anything between them, even if it hurt them both.

Closing his eyes, he leaned back against the mountain of pillows she insisted her bed needed, the same pillows she would throw on the floor throughout the night. Her sheets were outrageously soft and put his to shame. She hadn't uttered a peep of complaint the few times they had stayed at his place, but he could tell she hadn't slept as well there as she did here. Hell, he didn't sleep well at his place either, not after experiencing her setup.

A sharp pang of guilt struck him. It was so easy to just stay with her every night, to wake up with her and share their morning. It felt good. It felt like he finally belonged.

Yet, he wondered if she ever worried that he was taking advantage of her. The disparity in their finances was known to everyone. He would never be able to earn the kind of money she had inherited or the amount of it that she would eventually earn working in the firm. Forever and always, he would be poor compared to her.

He believed her when she said the differences in their bank accounts didn't matter. More than once, she had reminded him that she wasn't looking for a sugar daddy. She wanted a partner. She wanted someone she could trust. She wanted someone who loved her.

And he did love her. He had from the first moment she had grinned at him while driving like a madwoman in that stolen Camaro. She had stolen his heart that wild night, and as long as she wanted him, he was standing right beside her.

Looking around her room, he wondered, not for the first time, if he should suggest they find a different place together. Something smaller, easier to maintain. Something they could both afford so he could feel like he was contributing equally to their relationship. Some place that didn't have all these ghosts and memories for her.

The door to the bathroom opened, and he glanced over to ask her if she wanted to watch one of the home improvement shows she liked so much, but the question died on his lips. He had expected her to emerge in one of her favorite oversized and well-worn tees, but she was naked. He drew his gaze down her incredible body, letting it linger on the two ties dangling from her right hand.

Sitting up, he swung his legs over the edge of the bed, but she wagged her finger. "Stay."

He swallowed hard. "I thought we weren't…?"

"You promised me I could drive, remember?" Her lush hips swayed seductively as she crossed the floor and came to stand in front of him. She had loosely braided her hair to the side, and the ends of it draped over her breast, just hiding her nipple.

"I remember." He grasped her waist and welcomed her between his widened thighs. Even though he was already hard and aching for her, he still took a moment to check in with her. "Are you sure, Aston? We don't have to—"

She touched her perfectly manicured finger to his lips. "I want you."

He regarded her for a moment. Her eyes were clear and honest. She wasn't standing here, naked and willing, out of some sense of duty. She wanted him right now. She needed a good, hard fuck—and he was going to give it to her.

"Those ties for me or you?" he asked as his hands swept up and down her sides before settling on her hips.

"You."

Heat flared low in his belly as he imagined being tied down while she had her way with him. He had always been the more dominant in bed with her, taking and giving as he pleased. The idea of having to beg her for a taste of her mouth or the feel of her slick pussy taking him deep was enough to make him shudder with anticipation.

It occurred to him that his excitement at being restrained for her enjoyment stemmed from his deep trust in her. After what they had survived together that first night, he had known she was the sort of ride-or-die girl he had always dreamed of finding. No matter what, she would always have his back and he would always have hers.

"I'm too big for you to manhandle." He glanced at the ties in her hand. "Tell me where you want me."

She glanced around the room. Her gaze settled on the white leather bench at the foot of her bed. It wasn't too tall or too low. It was wide and padded enough to be comfortable. For a little while, at least.

"Okay." He stood and walked over to the bench. He pulled it away from the bed to give them plenty of room to play. After taking off his shirt, he stepped out of the loose pajama pants that already felt too restricting. Wanting to tease her a little, he asked, "On my stomach or on my back?"

Her eyes widened. "Um, maybe we try the simple stuff this first time?"

"Back it is," he agreed and settled into position. "Arms up? Or down?"

She teethed her bottom lip. "I want you to be comfortable so we can have fun."

"Arms up," he decided.

She knelt next to his head and gently pulled his arms down into position. She used a tie to lash each wrist to the legs of the bench. He tested the ties with a short tug and realized she hadn't secured him tightly enough to hinder his escape. He glanced at her and caught the worry in her expression.

"Baby, look at me." He waited until she met his gaze. "You

can't hurt me."

"I could," she said, seemingly on the edge of changing her mind about all of this.

"You really couldn't," he assured her. "I'm a lot sturdier than you. Unless you plan to Annie Wilkes me, we're fine."

She frowned. "Who is Annie Wilkes?"

"She's a character in a Stephen King novel. She has a sledgehammer, and she—"

Aston held up her hand to stop him. "I don't like scary books or movies," she reminded him.

"I know." Tired of talking, he said, "Get over here and fuck me."

"Ben!" Her scandalized smile and blushing face made his cock ache. He loved this side of her, the sweet little socialite who wanted to fuck dirty but still had that ingrained embarrassment that tried to hold her back.

"Would it be easier for you to use me like your favorite sex toy if I'm blindfolded?"

"No, but gagging you might help," she replied with an imperious look.

"There it is," he said with a laugh. "Let out your inner domme. Climb on top and wreck me."

"You are terrible." She grinned down at him, bending low to kiss him. "You're a terrible, naughty, bad boy," she said, her voice husky and dark. "And I'm going to punish you for it."

Ben's mouth gaped as he stared up at her in shock. He had been teasing about the domme thing, but hearing her talk like that made his dick throb. He could picture her in black leather or latex and thigh high boots, wielding a crop or paddle and ordering him around like a dog. There hadn't ever been anyone he could imagine submitting to, but Aston? He'd crawl across broken glass for the chance to bury his face between her legs.

Her touches were light and unsure at first, her fingers gliding over his arms and upper chest in a way that made his skin prickle. She grew bolder as she relaxed into the game they were playing. He closed his eyes and enjoyed the sensations her hands evoked as they moved over him, sliding over his jaw and neck and then lower to his stomach and navel.

When she straddled him, he exhaled a shaky breath. It was harder than he had imagined to sit perfectly still, arms bound above him and unable to reach for her. She seated herself just above his cock, leaving his shaft nestled against the plump softness of her ass. Her pussy was hot and slick for him, the wet heat of her leaving a trail on him as she leaned down to kiss him.

But at the last second, she skipped his mouth. Her ticklish kisses dotted his face, lingering on his cheeks and chin and jaw. Once, she brushed the corner of his mouth, and he tried to turn and capture hers, but she moved away too quickly. He hissed when her tongue dragged down the surprisingly sensitive swath of his throat. She sucked hard just above his Adam's apple before moving even lower, nipping and scraping her teeth over his neck.

His entire body vibrated. She dotted more kisses and love bites along his chest before lifting up her hips and reaching down between their bodies to grasp him. Her soft hand clasped his cock, stroking it so slowly he groaned. Her mouth was on his suddenly, her kiss forceful and rough, completely different than the fleeting pecks from earlier. Her tongue stabbed against his, and she ran her hand up and down his shaft, a little tighter, a little faster.

She carefully pulled his dick forward, toward his navel, and then lowered her pussy against him. It was the kind of maddening contact that made him want to call an end to their game. He wanted to be inside her, thrusting up into her until his thighs burned, but she wouldn't let him. She moved forward, dragging the slick heat of her along the underside of his shaft. He was taken back to the frustrating years of teenage fumbling and experimenting. It felt good—so fucking good— but it wasn't enough.

And she knew it.

She liked having him on the verge of begging. Her gaze had gone smoky and dark. Hovering over him, torturing him with her sweet cunt, she looked different. She was more flushed than he had ever seen her. Her nipples looked bigger, darker, and he could see the bluish green shadow of veins just under her skin. He hadn't ever noticed them before and would have put more thought into why but she started to talk and he damn near lost his mind.

"I saw a toy the other day." She rubbed her clit against the head of his cock. A hint of a smile crossed her face as he flexed and tried to arch underneath her. "It was a sleeve that goes over you right here." She rubbed along the full length of him, and his breath hitched. "It vibrates here," she touched the base of his shaft, "and here."

"Fuck," he growled as she ground her clit against the throbbing head.

"I thought about buying it. I thought about tying you up in my bed and leaving it on you while I work on my class assignments. It's wirelessly controlled. I could turn it up and down until I'm ready." She placed both hands on his chest and lifted her backside in the most torturously slow motion. When he felt the tip of his cock slide just inside her, he gritted his teeth and prayed he wouldn't come just yet. "How fast do you think I would come with your dick vibrating inside me?"

"Buy it," he growled. "Buy it, and you can do whatever the fuck you want with me. Just don't fucking move."

"Like this?" she asked, her face mocking him as she stood and stepped away from him.

"Aston!"

"Patience is a virtue," she replied in an annoying singsong voice. "Wait."

He didn't want to wait. He wanted her. Now.

"Oh, fuck," he groaned. Her hot mouth was suddenly on him. That wicked tongue of hers glided over him. She flicked at the sensitive spots she had discovered in their first wild nights together and sucked him in the way he liked the most. One of her hands played with his balls, and the other scratched lightly at his lower belly and chest. He couldn't focus on one sensation over the other. It all felt so fucking good. Her mouth, her hands—she was driving him fucking insane.

She hummed hungrily and slurped in the most unladylike way. The sound and feel of her mouth working on him had his toes curling into the thick rug at the base of her bed. His fingers were already tightened into fists, and he started to feel that warning coil low in his belly. He was so ready to come, to feel her swallowing down his cum. His breaths came in shaking pants, and he closed his eyes, anticipating the explosion to come.

But she stopped.

She fucking stopped.

"Aston! Fuck!" His shout echoed off the vaulted ceiling as his entire body tensed. He jerked against the ties. For a second, he thought about breaking them, about jumping to his feet and kicking away the bench before throwing her onto the bed and pounding into her. Inhaling a ragged breath, he pushed away the thought. This was her game. She was in charge.

In the next moment, she was straddling him again. She faced his feet this time and was too high up on his chest to mount him. It quickly occurred to him what she wanted. He grinned devilishly. A few times, he had tried to drag her onto his face like this, but she hadn't been able to relax and enjoy it. Apparently, she had overcome those issues tonight.

She leaned forward over him and pressed her pussy against his mouth. He didn't need any instructions from her. He knew what she wanted, and he was going to give it to her. She shuddered and moaned as his tongue traced her. Pressing back even more, she silently beckoned him to please her. He wasn't about to disappoint her.

He swirled his tongue and flicked and sucked at her, eating her like the juiciest fucking peach. She rewarded his effort with moans and whimpers. He teased her for a while, keeping his tongue everywhere except the one place she wanted it. When her hand moved over his cock with a featherlight stroke, he slid his tongue into place and fluttered it over the stiff nub there. She swore quietly and grasped his thigh, her short nails digging into his skin and marking him like the wildcat she was.

She stroked him with stuttering movements, her focus taken away by his mouth between her legs. Her thighs started to tense, and he could feel them squeezing against his shoulders and neck. Just when he thought she was close, she pulled away from his mouth for a few seconds, panting and clutching at his leg again. The real torture of having his hands restrained finally hit him. He wanted to grab her thighs, to pull her down on his face and hold her there while he made her come. He wanted her to go wild, to thrash and scream while begging him to let go, to stop licking her and making her come so hard.

She repeated her teasing motions, letting herself get close before jerking away from his mouth. He nipped at her thighs, kissing and sucking any part of her soft skin he could reach. After a few times of denying herself, she finally settled herself back into place and lowered her body until she was flat on top of him, her breasts against his belly, her cheek against his stiff cock.

It didn't take much to send her over the edge. He swirled his tongue around her clit before drawing it between his lips. She cried out his name and climaxed. Her strangled cries filled the room as she rocked against his mouth, taking everything he had to give and letting herself revel in the sheer bliss of it.

She sagged on top of him. The weight of her was nothing. He loved the way it felt to have her draped across him like a blanket, her lush body keeping his warm. His cock ached, and his balls were throbbing. All he could think about was being inside her, touching her, loving her.

"Untie me," he practically begged. "Let me fuck you, Aston."

She rose on shaking legs and knelt down to undo the makeshift restraints. He sat up quickly, blood rushing to his head, and shot to his feet. He didn't even give her a chance to stand fully before he reached down and lifted her from her kneeling position. She gasped at his show of strength and then giggled uncontrollably when he tossed her onto the bed. She bounced on the big bed and dropped back against it, parting her thighs and welcoming him to take her.

He climbed onto the bed and grabbed her hips. In a quick movement, he flipped her over, shocking her again with the use of his power. He was always keenly aware of how much bigger and stronger he was than her. He always tried to move deliberately with her, to treat her with care and not like some lumbering brute. Sometimes, though, he wanted her to feel the real strength of him. Like right now.

He dragged her up onto her knees and grabbed a handful of her braid, lifting her head and straightening her back. He waited a moment, uncertain whether she would tell him to loosen up or slow down or be more careful. The only word that came out of her mouth was a desperate, "Please."

If she expected him to thrust into her like some barbarian, she was disappointed. He teased her in the same way she had him. He gave her just the tip and then a little more and a little more until he finally bottomed out in her slick pussy. Her thighs were a mess, shining and wet.

His strokes were smooth and forceful at first. She met him stroke for stroke, her back arched beautifully and her chin high. He could easily imagine her in the role of submissive, graceful and delicate and eager to please. The possibilities between them were endless, and he couldn't wait to try them all.

Spurred on by her endless cries, he thrust harder and rougher. His hips moved in a steady rhythm, and soon, she was reaching between her legs and framing her clit with her fingers. He moved off both knees, lifting his right foot and planting it beside her to give him better leverage. She damn near squealed when he thrust at the new angle. "Ben. Ben. Ben. Ben!"

The flutter and squeeze of her pussy was enough to make his head explode. He lost control then, giving in to the animal side of him that demanded he fuck faster and harder. She screamed his name even louder, and he let go, letting his pent-up release flood out of him and into her.

When she collapsed forward onto the bed, he followed, dropping down on top of her in a sweaty heap of flesh and heat. He was too heavy to stay that way for long. Even though his tired muscles protested, he lifted up on his palms, arms flexing, and kissed a slow trail down her spine as he moved off of her. He rolled to the side and met her shy, almost nervous gaze. "Come here."

She moved into his waiting embrace, curling up against him and resting her head on his chest. She held onto him, one of her arms snaking under his and the other clutching at his hip. "Was that okay?"

At her soft, worried tone, he kissed her forehead. "That was way more than okay."

"I didn't hurt you?"

Amused by her concern but also loving her all the more for it, he smiled. "You didn't hurt me." He brushed loose, damp strands of hair from her face. "Did I hurt you? At the end?"

"No." She pressed her lips to his chest. "It was perfect."

They stayed like that for a while, stroking and petting gently while trading lazy kisses. Eye to eye, he cupped her cheek and nuzzled his nose against hers. "I love you, Aston."

She smiled. "I love you more."

"Impossible." He kissed her tenderly. "Utterly impossible."

She started to speak, but the unexpected ringing of the doorbell startled them both. Frowning, they sat up as the doorbell rang again and again. Someone wanted their attention.

"My phone," she said, reaching across him. He snatched it first from the bedside table and gave it to her. She opened the app that was connected to the security system. The doorbell camera gave them a view of the front door—and the police officers stacked one behind the other, ready to make entry.

Fuck.

CHAPTER TEN

"**G**ET DRESSED."

I shot a panicked look at Ben but did as he had ordered. His voice had morphed from tender and loving to deep and harsh. Irritation and anger vibrated off him in waves. He wasn't mad at me, of course. He was furious that the police were at my front door and probably thought it was his fault somehow.

"We'll be down in a minute," Ben snapped at my phone after activating the microphone one the security app.

"Sir, Houston PD. We have a warrant."

"I'm sure you do, but it's after fucking midnight. We have to get dressed."

Ben tossed the phone onto the bed and stormed over to his hastily discarded pajama bottoms and shirt. I ran into the closet, stopping just long enough to grab a towel to tidy up before pulling on the first pair of shorts and tee I found.

When I came back into the bedroom, Ben stood near the windows overlooking the front lawn. He had pulled back the blackout panels to reveal the blue and red flashing lights. Even from this distance, I could see his jaw clenching. He was angrier than I had ever seen him.

"Ben," I reached for his hand, "promise me you aren't going to punch a cop."

His scowl softened. "I promise."

"I mean it."

"I'm not doing anything that will take me away from you."
He kissed me hard. "When we get downstairs, stand away
from me. Don't put your hands in your pockets or behind you.
Keep them in view. No quick movements."

"Ben, they're not going to shoot us!"

"You don't know that," he insisted, his voice thick with
worry. "The police don't show up with flashing lights after
midnight in this part of town unless they're trying to send a
message. Do you understand how serious this is?"

I swallowed hard. Was he right? Was this some form of
intimidation? I didn't like to admit that I had certain privileges
that others in the city would never experience. I had never had
problems with the police. I had never been profiled or strong
armed or brutalized.

"You're right," I agreed. "Normally, the police would reach
out to me, have my lawyer get involved and arrange a time and
place for questioning or a search."

"Yes," he said, seemingly glad that I had accepted his view
of the situation. "Get your phone. Call your lawyer. Now."

"Right." I grabbed my phone from the bed and made the
call. Holding onto Ben's hand, I let him lead me out of the
bedroom and downstairs. He turned on lights as we moved,
letting the police follow our movements through the windows.
We had made it almost to the front door when my family's
longtime attorney answered.

"Hello?" A gruff and sleepy voice answered.

"Dick? It's Aston McNeil. I'm so sorry to be calling so late, but there are a bunch of police at my front door with a warrant. I don't know what to do."

"Jesus Christ," Dick grumbled in that Texas twang of his. "Hang on, Aston." There was shuffling in the background, and he seemed to be addressing his wife, Charlene. "Aston? You still there?"

"Yes."

"Answer the door. Ask to see the warrants. Don't let them in until you've read them. Tell them your legal team is on their way."

"Okay." I beckoned Ben to move out of the way, but he refused to let me open the door. His shoulders squared, his stance defensive, he stepped forward and unlocked the door. He seemed ready to take whatever brunt of violence might be bursting through the door at any moment.

"Aston McNeil?"

"No," Ben practically snarled.

"Mr. Beciraj?" Detective Dawson appeared in the doorway. His easy, gentle smile from the other morning was gone. Now, he was all business. "Can you step aside?"

"Wait," I said, rushing forward and drawing a frustrated glance from Ben. "My legal team is on their way. I need to see the warrants first. Please," I added, softening my expression to show I wanted to cooperate.

Detective Dawson stretched out his hand. "Here."

I took the folded papers from him and began to read them. I took my time, reading each word carefully as I tried to make sense of why the police were at my door. The police stared on in exasperation, their irritation with being forced to stand outside growing. When I reached the end of the second warrant, I frowned and met Detective Dawson's stony gaze. "This is an arrest warrant for Calvin and a search warrant for my house—where I expressly told you that my stepbrother wasn't welcome and hadn't visited in weeks."

"You wouldn't be the first sister to hide a family member she swears she hates and hasn't seen in years," the detective replied. "We have to find him. The sooner you let us inside to search, the faster we'll be out of your hair."

"I don't understand how you convinced a judge to give you a search warrant to look for a man in a house where he hasn't lived in more than ten years." Still blocking the door, I turned my attention to the papers again and studied the signatures. "Judge Garland? He signed this? He signed this knowing it was Calvin you're looking for? In my house?"

Detective Dawson briefly averted his gaze. "Yes."

I narrowed my eyes at him. "I don't believe you."

"Believe what you want," he countered, "but we are coming inside. It will be better for everyone if you step aside."

"Or what? You're going to arrest me?" Knowing that they had somehow fooled elderly Judge Garland, one of my father's favorite golf buddies, into signing this piece of crap warrant made me angry. The judge had been the one who helped my father and stepmother find a private school that would take Calvin after he had been expelled from every school in the city. Judge Garland had been the one who had suggested my stepmother have Calvin evaluated by a team of psychiatrists so he could be locked away where he wouldn't be able to hurt anyone.

He was also nearly ninety years old and on the cusp of finally retiring. The invitation to the retirement party his wife was hosting was on my desk. The word at the country club where we all played golf was that he had been diagnosed with some kind of memory problem—dementia or Alzheimer's. He hadn't been handling cases, just occupying a seat until he reached the milestone retirement date he had set for himself.

"Aston," Ben warned softly, his big hand settling on my shoulder in a reassuring way.

Exhaling slowly, I looked the detective square in the eye. "You know what? Go head. Come in here and search my house. You won't find anything. And me? I'm going to call Judge Garland. Or, maybe I'll just walk six doors down to the end of the cul-de-sac where he lives and ring his doorbell?" At that, the detective blanched. "The judge is a very old family friend, and he knows all about Calvin. I'm sure he'll be able to explain to me why he signed this warrant. I'm sure it's all perfectly legal and ethical."

Detective Dawson hesitated. He seemed to realize he had overplayed his hand. Maybe he wasn't the one who got the judge to sign the warrant. Maybe it had been someone else in his department. Still, the ax would come down on his neck. Once Dick arrived and realized what was happening, he would go ballistic.

Stepping aside, I let them in with a flourish of my arm. "Be my guest, gentlemen."

Ben's jaw tensed as he moved closer to me. He had one hand on my waist and shifted his body in a way that shielded me from the stream of police officers and crime scene techs walking through the door. Leaning down, he whispered, "You sure about this?"

Lifting the warrants to cover my mouth, I answered just as

quietly, "The judge who signed these is senile. There's no way any of this is legal. You were right." I glanced up at him. "They're here to send a message. They're trying to scare me."

"They fucking failed," he murmured, drawing me closer. Glad to share in his strength, I leaned against him while we watched police officers march through the house. I wasn't worried about anyone trying to take anything. Anything worth taking was hidden away in safes, and the security system had cameras in everywhere but the bathrooms and my bedroom, all of them recording and storing their data on the cloud.

"Ben."

We both turned toward the detective who had come through the door last. Ben immediately stiffened, and I could tell there was some history between the two men. The handsome detective had dark hair and eyes, but there was something sad about him, something sorrowful in his eyes.

"Santos." Ben addressed him by his last name. "The fuck are you doing here?"

"I could ask you the same thing." Detective Santos looked around the house. "Not really your usual scene, is it? Not a stripper pole or G-string to be seen."

If he thought that I wasn't aware that Ben's family was heavily invested in gentlemen's clubs, he was mistaken. I didn't even bat an eye. I held the detective's gaze as I outstretched my hand. "Aston McNeil. I don't think we've met."

"We haven't." He grasped my hand with a strong shake. "Eric Santos. Detective. Guns and Gangs."

"Uh-huh," I said, unimpressed.

"I'm not here for you," he remarked, his steady gaze back on Ben. "But your stepbrother is of interest to me."

"You're not going to find him here."

Eric's gaze shifted to me. "We'll see."

"Is he always like that?" I asked as the detective walked away and disappeared into my father's study.

"Yes." Ben pressed a tender kiss to the top of my head. "I'm sorry."

"Don't be."

"He's trying to rattle me, too." He lowered his voice. "The noodle shop."

"Oh," I whispered, finally understanding.

It wasn't long before the sound of car doors being slammed echoed outside. Within moments, the legal cavalry stormed through the front door. A few of the younger ones seemed to have been working late on the weekend, their suits rumpled and not as crisp as they should have been. The older attorneys had arrived in lounge wear—leggings and yoga pants on the three women—and jeans for the two older men, including an apoplectic Dick.

"What in the Sam Hill is going on here?" Dick shouted, his deep voice echoing off the vaulted ceilings of the entryway and the marble floors. "Who the hell is in charge of this goat rope?"

I didn't even try to hide my smile. Dick was known as one of the best criminal defense attorneys in the country. He had become a bit of a celebrity with his winning defenses of high-profile murder cases, but while he had conquered the city, he had never forgotten where he came from—a dusty ranch in far west Texas.

"You three get upstairs and make sure these cretins aren't rifling through her underwear drawer," he snapped, pointing at the younger lawyers. "Rosie, Hank, take the office," he commanded, gesturing to the correct door. "Sugar," Dick said, noticing me finally. He swept in and clamped a bear paw on my shoulder. "You all right?"

"I'm fine. Just confused," I said, looking at the police officers who had stopped searching to stare. "They gave me these."

Dick took the warrants and scanned them. His face got redder and his jaw clenched as he read through them. "Look at this horseshit, Mariana."

I recognized her as one of the partners of his firm. Even though she was in black leggings and a Baylor sweater, she looked effortlessly classic. She glanced over the warrants and rolled her eyes. "Garland?"

"Yeah," Dick grumbled, his gaze moving to Detective Dawson who seemed less than enthusiastic about talking to him. "Dawson! You must be dumb as a box of rocks if you think this will stand up!"

"Good to see you, too, Dick," Detective Dawson greeted sarcastically. "They're good warrants."

"Bullshit," Dick snapped. "Everyone knows Garland is a few sandwiches short of a picnic. Hell, last week, the old fool got lost trying to find the bathrooms and whipped his pecker out in the hall outside Karen Gonzalez's chambers to water a fake ficus. He's just warming a seat until he retires." Dick narrowed his eyes. "But, you knew that, didn't you? You went to him because your crack team knew there wasn't enough to get a sane judge to sign this shit."

"It wasn't my team that secured the warrants," Detective Dawson insisted. "I'm just doing what I was told."

"Is there a problem?" Detective Santos interjected as he

stepped up beside Dawson who shot him an angry look. It was clear from their exchanged glances that Dawson felt as if he had been set up to fail.

"Hell, I should have known this was your handiwork, Eric," Dick said with a harsh laugh. "Another one of your tricks, huh? You're always working some angle. What is it this time? Trying to bully this girl into being your next informant? Huh? You want her to end up floating in Trinity Bay with her throat slit and tongue cut out like the last one?"

Eric bristled. "What happened to Carrie—"

"Is not happening to my client," Dick snarled. "I've been in Aston's life since she was a baby. Her daddy was one of my best friends. You picked the wrong girl to intimidate."

"Listen," Dawson tried to intervene, "I'm sure we can talk about this and find a compromise."

"Dawson, you couldn't find the goddamn floor if you fell out of bed," Dick shouted.

Dick's raised voice must have startled one of the crime scene techs on the staircase. She turned quickly, and her camera strap caught onto the edge of the sunburst mirror frame. It clattered as it bounced against a step and shattered, sending glass shards down the staircase and onto the floor. She blanched, and I felt terrible for her. It was just a mirror, but she had made herself a target of Dick's ire.

"Get the hell out of this house before I have you all fired!"

The techs and police officers who had gathered to watch the fireworks looked between Dick and the detectives. After a tense moment, Eric jerked his head. The investigative team all but ran to the doors where two of the lawyers who had come with Dick stood guard, stopping and interrogating them.

When the woman who had caused the mirror to fall walked by, I reached out to touch her arm. She winced, as if expecting me to yell at her for breaking it. I just smiled. "Hey, don't worry about the mirror. It was an accident."

"I'm really sorry," she said. "I've never done something like that on a scene."

"It happens. It's fine." I waved my hand. "It was on clearance at Kirkland's. It's not a big deal."

She seemed relieve to hear that it wasn't some priceless antique. With a nod, she scurried toward the door and avoided Dick's glare.

Detective Dawson was the second to last to leave. He didn't say a word as he escaped the house. Eric Santos, however, wasn't about to disappear without getting in a few parting shots.

"We're going to find Calvin, Miss McNeil. We're going to find him and Gary and get to the bottom of this fucked up scheme you've got going."

Before I could protest, he was gone. I glanced at Dick and he shook his head, silently warning me not to speak just yet. He stepped aside to talk to his team. Most of them left, but Rosie and Mariana stayed behind, both of them on their phones typing furiously.

"I'm going to clean up the glass." Ben rubbed my lower back and eyed my bare feet. "Be careful."

"I will."

As Ben walked away, Dick touched my arm. "We need to talk."

I nodded. "Dad's office?"

"Sure."

When we were safely locked inside, I walked straight to the bar cart and grabbed a glass. "You want one?"

"Like I'm going to pass up the chance to sip on your daddy's Pappy Van Winkle collection?" He dropped into one of the chesterfield chairs near the fireplace. "You got yourself a hell of a mess here, kid."

"I know." I poured some of the bourbon into each glass and handed him one before taking the seat across from him. "I really don't know what the detective meant about Calvin and Gary."

Dick sipped his bourbon. "He talking about Gary Metcalfe?"

"I think so. Why? Do you know something?"

"I was at the golf course this morning, and I heard some scuttlebutt about some money going missing. Gary's name was mentioned. How does he tie in to you?"

"His wife works for the firm." I took a drink. "She walked out in tears earlier this week. Apparently, a federal agent came to see her at work. When I was at Oliver's wedding tonight, I heard her house had been raided."

"Ollie, that old romantic," he said with a huffed laugh. "He's singlehandedly keeping the prenup and divorce lawyers in business."

"He has a good heart," I insisted. "He's just unlucky in love."

Dick grumbled and sat back in the chair. "Tell me what I need to know."

I explained the visit from Detective Dawson and what I had pieced together from conversations since then.

"And Ben Beciraj?" He eyed me in a way that made me

squirm. "How does he fit into all this?"

"We're dating."

"And?"

"And what?" I shrugged. "We're together. End of story."

"I have a feeling that's the beginning of the story," he replied. "How the hell does a man like that meet someone like you?"

Knowing Dick would never betray my confidence, I told him the truth. "Calvin was in money trouble. He used Baby to get a loan from Ben's family. They repossessed the car. I went to Ben to demand it back, and we spent the night running from drug dealers and car thieves and loan sharks. We've been together ever since."

"Jesus Christ." He finished off his bourbon in one long pull. "You get all that settled?"

"Yes."

"The drug dealers were tied in with Calvin?" he guessed.

"Yes."

"And that's been handled? You're safe?"

"I'm safe. It was handled."

He sighed and set his glass on the table next to him. He sat forward and leaned his elbows on his knees. "Do you know where Calvin is?"

I met his gaze and shook his head. "No."

"Do you know why he's missing?"

I swallowed nervously. "Yes."

"Is he going to come back and cause any problems?"

I shook my head.

"I see." He had obviously had enough criminals in front of him to know what I was saying without saying it. "Good." He seemed to relax as he straightened up. "There's a lot you don't know about that little shit. Things he did to animals. Things he did to girls he dated," he added. "Things he did to boys at the military academy. Things no one could prove because his victims wouldn't or couldn't talk to police."

"I didn't know," I murmured, feeling even worse that my stepbrother had been out there hurting people all that time.

"Your daddy did. Maybe not to the extent I knew, but he had an idea of what that monster was like. I told him to take that rotten asshole on a hunting trip and give him the Dick Cheney treatment."

My eyes widened at the idea of my dad "accidentally" shooting Calvin in the face during a hunt.

"Sometimes, you got to cull the herd, sweetheart. That boy was a bad seed from the moment he took hold in his mama's belly." He stood up. "He was going to end up in an unmarked grave or at the bottom of the bay eventually," Dick said matter-of-factly. "He just hadn't crossed the wrong person yet." His gaze flicked to the closed door. "Or, rather, you hadn't met the right one yet."

Dick had gotten the answers he needed, and I walked him to the front door where the rest of his team waited patiently, all of them head down and focused on their phones. "You have any more problems, you call me."

"I will."

"The team will be in touch Monday morning. We'll get this sorted."

"Thank you for coming tonight. I'm really sorry I had to wake all of you."

"You won't be when you get the bill," Dick replied with his

trademark grin.

He was probably right about that. I waited until they were gone to lock the door behind them. Leaning back against it, I sighed heavily. Ben appeared in the entryway, a vacuum in hand. "Everyone gone?"

"Yes."

"Let me finish cleaning this up, and we'll go back to bed?"

"Sounds good."

While Ben vacuumed, I wandered back to Dad's study and started closing drawers and cabinets that had been left open by the police. The house felt weirdly violated, and I couldn't shake the feeling that it might not ever feel like my safe place again.

My gaze fell to the spot where Ben had almost killed Calvin. I didn't worry about evidence being found. Ben had hired someone—a professional who handled only underworld clients—to clean the house and wipe away every trace.

But the cleaner he had hired couldn't wipe away the memory.

Ben stepped into the study. "You okay?"

"Not really," I confessed, feeling suddenly overwhelmed.

"Baby," he murmured and closed the distance between us with long strides. When his strong arms gathered me close, I sagged against him. I closed my eyes and pressed my cheek to his chest, letting the soothing thud of his heartbeat calm me. He didn't try to fill the silence with empty platitudes or promises. He just held me and stroked my hair, giving me exactly what I needed.

A long time later, when I felt a little better, I stared up at him. "I think that mirror breaking was a sign."

"Of what?" His thumb followed the curve of my jaw. "You don't believe in that seven years of bad luck shit, right?"

"No."

"But?"

"But I've been thinking that it's time to downsize."

He seemed surprised. "You want to sell your house?"

"Do you think that's a bad decision?"

"No. I have been thinking about talking to you about it." He hesitated. "This place is becoming a mausoleum, Aston."

"I know."

"You can make new memories somewhere else. Maybe you don't even have to sell it. You could close it down and move and decide what to do about it later."

"That's a possibility I hadn't considered. Yeah. Maybe."

"What about Nina and Pedro?"

"They've been talking about retiring."

"Are they okay? Like financially?"

"Dad had them on a retirement plan, and he left them money in his will. Enough to let them travel and spoil their grandkids and great-grandkids and leave trust funds for them all."

"He must have cared about them."

"They're family."

Ben kissed me. "Let's go back to bed. We can figure this all out tomorrow."

"It's already tomorrow," I pointed out.

"Fine. Later today?"

"Much later," I agreed and took hold of his hand. As I led him upstairs, I felt a strange lightening sensation. Maybe I would sell the house. Maybe I wouldn't. Either way, it was time to make some changes in my life.

But not with Ben. He was the constant, steady presence that belonged right next to me.

CHAPTER ELEVEN

WHEN BEN FINALLY made it downstairs the next morning, he discovered Aston holding a spatula in one hand while staring at a smoking griddle. Certain she was on the brink of burning the whole damn house down, he said, "Step away from the stove."

Startled by his sudden appearance, Aston spun around to glare at him. "You almost gave me a heart attack!"

"Sorry." Reaching around her, he quickly shut off the burners under the cast iron griddle.

"It needs to heat up," she protested.

"Baby, it's smoking."

"Isn't it supposed to do that? How else do I know if it's hot enough?"

He bit back a laugh. Instead of telling her that there was such a thing as too hot, he wrapped his arms around her from behind and kissed her neck. She relaxed back against him as he dotted slow kisses along her exposed skin. She still had that slightly sleepy, rumpled look about her. The little shorts she wore had him thinking about everything but breakfast. Unless she was offering herself up to be eaten, of course.

"I can make pancakes," she insisted. "See? I already mixed the batter."

He eyed the too thick and lumpy glop in the bowl next to the stove. "You mixed something up," he agreed, "but I've seen concrete thinner than that."

She elbowed him hard enough to make him wince. "Rude."

Laughing, he kissed her neck again. "Let me handle this. You go make coffee."

"Fine." She acted as if she were upset that he was pushing her away from the stove, but he could tell she was relieved. She had tried, and that was enough for him.

He carried the bowl of batter to the sink and added a little more water. He alternated whisking with adding water until the batter reached the correct consistency. Shaking his head, he decided it was a good thing she was so fucking rich. She would starve to death if she had to cook for herself.

"They have couples cooking lessons." She placed a cup of coffee next to him and watched as he ladled circles of pancake batter onto the hot griddle.

He waited to see if she was going to ask him if he wanted to go with her. When she didn't, he set aside the ladle and picked up the cup of coffee. There was a melting ice cube floating in it, just the way he liked. He hated having to wait to drink his coffee until it cooled. After a sip, he asked, "Do you want to go together?"

"Do you?" She seemed apprehensive as she stared up at him.

"Aston, I'll go anywhere you tell me to go," he replied matter-of-factly. "You want to go to cooking class? We'll go to cooking class. You want me to take you to the ballet? I'll get tickets. You want me to sit with you through one of those four-hour-long operas? I'll buy some ear plugs."

She snorted with laughter. "I'll look into it. The cooking classes, not the opera," she clarified. "I had no idea you hated it so much."

"I'm not a fan of concerts or clubs or bars," he admitted. "Too fucking loud. Gives me a headache." He noticed she was drinking hot tea instead of coffee and frowned. "When did you start drinking tea with breakfast?"

"I'm trying something different. My stomach has been a mess the last few days. I think I need to clean up my diet."

He suspected there was something more to her stomach problems than her food choices. The stress she was under with school, work and now all of this legal shit was enough to send most people into a breakdown. Worried about her, he flipped the pancakes and considered what he could to do to help her relax.

"You want to go on vacation?" he asked when she returned to his side with two plates.

Clearly surprised by his question, she nodded and then grinned. "Yes. I would love to go away with you."

"Where?" He transferred pancakes to the plates and ladled the remaining batter onto the griddle. "I know we can't go away for a long time because of your class schedule and work, but maybe we could sneak out of town on a Thursday night and come back on Sunday evening?"

"Do you have a passport?"

"Yes."

"That gives us a lot of options. Or," she said, leaving his side to grab forks, "we could stay stateside. Maybe California? There's so many romantic getaway spots there."

"I've never been to California." He flipped pancakes. "If you can find something that you like, we'll go. My treat," he added, pinning her with a look.

"Fine with me."

As he plated the last of the pancakes, the doorbell rang. They exchanged nervous glances, and he shut off the burners. "I'll get it. You stay here."

Gripping a fork like a weapon, she nodded. "Okay."

As he strode across the house, barefoot without a shirt and in just gym shorts, he hoped he wasn't going to have to brawl with someone. After last night, there was no telling what kind of bullshit was on the other side of the door right now.

"Oh. It's you." Ben said, more relieved than irritated, as he discovered Besian on the welcome mat.

"Don't sound so happy to see me, Ben." Besian frowned and removed his aviator sunglasses, tucking them into the open collar of his shirt.

Ben gestured for him to come inside. "We had unwanted visitors last night."

"I heard." Besian looked him over, as if searching for bruises or injuries. "You both okay?"

"Aston's lawyer handled it."

"Good."

"Santos was here," he said, certain the boss would want to know that.

"I figured," Besian grumbled.

"You want some pancakes?"

Besian shook head. "I wouldn't say no to a cup of coffee."

When they entered the kitchen, Aston had taken up a perch on one of the white leather barstools at the marble island. She smiled as Besian appeared behind him. "Hey you!"

"Hello." Besian hadn't quite gotten comfortable with Aston's friendliness yet. "I hope it's all right if I stay for a bit?"

"Sure. You want pancakes?"

"No. Coffee?"

She stabbed her fork in the direction of the coffee bar. "Make yourself at home."

Enjoying the sight of Besian perturbed at being told to make his own coffee, Ben slipped onto the stool next to Aston. She didn't know—or maybe she did—that Besian was used to being served by women. It was his default setting to assume that she would hop off her seat and hurry to make him a cup. Later, the boss would probably have a comment about that. Not that he cared any.

"Is that Isaia?" Aston asked as she slathered a shocking amount of butter on her pancakes. She normally didn't eat much, if any, butter, but this morning, she appeared to be craving it.

"This?" Besian touched his suit as he waited for his coffee cup to fill. "Yes."

"It's a great fit. That color is fantastic on you. Much better than the Brioni windowpane you had on the last time I saw you," she remarked matter-of-factly.

Besian narrowed his eyes. "I like that Brioni."

"I'm sure you do," she replied with a shrug. "Doesn't mean it's the right suit for you."

Besian glanced at him, and Ben avoided his glare. "Are there any other items of clothing you think I should pull out of my closet?"

"I've never seen your closet, but if you let me in there, I bet

I'd find a few things that need to go."

"Is she always like this?" Besian asked before grabbing his cup of coffee from the machine.

"Yes." Ben smiled at her. "Always."

"I used to shop for my dad," she explained as Besian took a seat across from them. "He was built like you. Tall, lean but defined muscle," she added and gestured toward him with her fork. "You should stay away from windowpane and pinstripes. Stick to greys and blues. Maybe try some lavender or pink solid shirts. They'll look nice against your hair and eyes."

"I'll keep that in mind," he grumbled and sipped his coffee.

"Pink is Marley's favorite color," she said offhandedly. "Just, you know, a fact you might need some time. Not neon pink, though. She likes the softer shades. Like peonies."

Ben smirked at her obvious hints.

Besian didn't take the bait and ask about Marley. Instead, he cleared his throat and reached into his jacket to retrieve folded papers. He slid them across the counter. "I got these from Alina this morning. She's the one who told me about the police trouble you had."

"It was bluster," Aston assured him. "Dick ran them out of here with their tails tucked between their legs."

"They'll be back," Besian warned. "Especially Eric. He's tenacious. He'll grab onto you like a Pit Bull and sling you around by the neck until you break."

"That's a lovely image," she groused and turned her attention back to her pancakes.

Shooting Besian an annoyed look, Ben snatched the papers. The last thing Aston needed was more fuel for her anxiety and stress. He opened the folded papers and quickly thumbed through them. The first was a photo of the man who had died in the front seat of the red truck. Paul Chen. Twenty-nine. Chinese American.

"I know him," Aston said and grabbed the paper from his hands. "He was a TA in my stats courses." She stared down at his driver's license photo. "Why do you have this?"

"He was one of the men who died at Phan's," Besian explained. "In the red truck."

"Did you go to the pawn shop?" Ben asked.

"I did." Besian's expression made it clear that he didn't want to be asked about Marley. "The video had a clear shot of the driver. It was Gary Metcalfe." Besian's gaze landed on Aston. "His wife works with you?"

She nodded, her focus still on the photo of Paul Chen. "For now."

Ben raised an eyebrow at that reply. "What happened to standing up for her?"

"I will," she confirmed, "but, ultimately, that decision ends with Oliver. I'm not the CEO. He is."

"For now," Ben parroted her early reply.

She tapped the paper she held. "So how are Gary and Paul tied together? Paul was working on his doctorate when I knew him. Something crazy complicated in math."

"He was handling imports out of a small office on Harwin," Besian said. "It's on the third page."

Ben found it and handed it to her. While she looked over the information, he turned back to Besian. "Where did Alina get this?"

"Her lawyer has been digging. She lost some money, and

she's not happy."

Alina's temper was legendary. She looked sweet and kind, but under that beautiful exterior was a woman who would burn your house down with you tied up inside it. If she felt wronged, she would go for the jugular.

"Paul was doing all of his import business in Asia, mostly Hong Kong and Macau," Aston said thoughtfully. "Ben, when Detective Dawson came to see me at work, he was really keen on Asia. He asked me about Calvin traveling there and whether our firm has any offices there." She paused. "You know, Calvin gambled there. *A lot.* My dad and stepmom had to get him out of a really bad mess once. Like calling in favors and flying out to China in the middle of the night kind of situation. They wouldn't ever tell me anything about it. I always had the feeling dad had to cross one of his moral lines to handle it."

"There's a heavy Chinese presence on Harwin, right?" Ben tried to recreate that section of the city in his mind. "Some libraries and schools and shit like that?"

"There is," Besian confirmed. He hesitated, his gaze lingering on Aston before he finally said, "There have been some indications that there might be an unknown presence trying to push its way into the city."

Ben didn't need any other clues to put a name to what Besian suggested. "Triad?"

The boss nodded stiffly. "Possibly."

Aston's eyes widened. "That's, like, the Chinese mafia, right?"

"Yes." He and Besian both answered simultaneously.

Aston's expression turned pensive. "Maybe that's the tie?

Between Calvin, Gary and Paul. Maybe Calvin got in trouble with the Chinese mafia, right? And then he comes back home and he meets Gary because of the real estate his mom left to him in her will. He probably realized there was a way to use Gary to make money." Her voice trailed away as she looked through the papers again. "What if Gary's business is a front for money laundering?"

"Why do you think that?" he asked, loving the way her mind worked and feeling proud of her for jumping right on the problem.

"Because so many of Gary's clients are Chinese. See?" She placed one of the pages down on the counter. Her finger followed the column of names. "Look at how many there are."

"But what about these? These are all Latino," he said, noting the names.

"Portuguese," she corrected. "Macau was owned by Portugal until the late nineties. It was similar to Hong Kong and the British," she murmured as if her brain was running ahead to another thought. "Look at the dates of these clients handing their money to Gary. It's like a pattern. One Portuguese name in and two Chinese names out. This company sold a property and placed their money with Gary. They roll the funds to avoid taxes on capital gains. All legal," she added quickly. "Then they buy from these two companies. See?"

"Yeah."

"What was Paul importing?" Aston asked Besian. "That has to be the missing piece, right? Was it drugs?" She glanced at Ben. "That's what Calvin was screwing around with, wasn't he?"

"He was," Ben agreed, "but he wasn't buying from any

Chinese dealers. He was buying from the cartel."

"Would they be his competitors? If he wanted to push his way into business here?" she wondered. "Maybe it was some kind of market research? Trying to figure out what the competition was in Houston?"

"I'm not sure if Paul was importing drugs." Besian drank his coffee and cleared his throat again, as if debating whether or not to include Aston in what he was going to say next. "I think he might have been importing people, specifically young girls and boys."

Aston blinked. "Trafficking?"

"Yes," Besian confirmed soberly. "We've had a problem with it for a while. There's an unwritten rule in this city that snything to do with kids is absolutely a death sentence."

"But someone still has the balls to break those rules," she said quietly. "And you think that Gary Metcalfe can tell us if Paul and Calvin were in on some kind of Chinese mafia takeover of the city?"

"I do."

Aston chewed her lower lip. "There's only one way to draw him out."

Ben wasn't surprised she had come to that conclusion. He had the same one.

"We aren't going to hurt them," Besian assured gently. "If we can find his wife and baby and hold them somewhere safe, he'll come to us."

"You're going to kidnap them as collateral," she said bluntly. "You're going to use them as bait."

"That's the plan." Besian clearly wasn't thrilled by the idea of it, but he had come to terms with the necessity of it.

"And if she's already being held by someone else?" Aston asked.

"Like?"

"The FBI," Ben suggested, remembering the gossip at the wedding. "Their house was raided yesterday."

Besian drained the last of his coffee and stood up. "Then Gary Metcalfe is a dead man."

CHAPTER TWELVE

"**G**ET IN BEST bitch!" Marley greeted with a playful grin from behind the wheel of her Prius.

I laughed and settled into the passenger seat. I dropped my purse on the floorboard and reached for the seatbelt. "I'm glad it's your turn to drive."

"Tired?" she guessed, waiting for me to click my belt into place before putting her car in drive.

"Yep." I leaned back against the seat and looked at her outfit. She had paired a long-sleeved steel grey crop top with high waisted jeans and black boots. "That crop top is cute as hell."

"It's Nasty Gal. Grabbed it on sale last week," she added. "I figured our weekly Target run was a good time to wear it."

"I couldn't find anything to wear," I grumbled and gestured at my basic black leggings and Rice University tee.

"I've seen your closet. You could lose a small child in there. How do you have nothing to wear?"

"I'm bloated." I poked my pudgy stomach and frowned. "I tried to fasten my favorite pair of jeans and almost passed out because they were so tight. Even these leggings feel too small."

Obviously not believing me, Marley eyed me more critically. "You haven't gained weight in, like, five years. Why would you start now?"

"Maybe it's that happy fat thing?"

"Happy what thing?"

"Happy fat," I repeated. "It's when you get comfortable in a relationship and start to pack on pounds."

"You're at the gym five mornings a week."

"I must be eating more calories than I'm burning. This whole week I ate like absolute shit."

"I guess," Marley replied, unconvinced. A moment later as we idled at a stop sign, she asked, "Is it just your belly that's bloated? What about your boobs?"

I glared down at them. "They're spilling out of my bras. I was lucky my dress last night had a little extra room in it."

"Do they hurt?"

"Sometimes, yeah," I said, wondering what she was thinking.

"You were nauseated yesterday morning at the gym?"

"Yeah. So?"

"Does any of your food taste weird?"

I shrugged. "I had some champagne that tasted bitter last night. Ben said his was fine."

"And, uh, when was your last period?"

Finally realizing what she was insinuating, I exclaimed, "I am not pregnant!"

"Are you sure? Did you take a test?"

"I had a period, like, three weeks ago. It was a few days late, but it came."

"A normal period? Like, I'm sorry for being so TMI, but did you bleed the same amount?"

"No," I admitted reluctantly. "It was short and mostly

spotting."

"Okay, well, we are buying a pregnancy test at Target," Marley decided. "Because what if that was implantation spotting?"

"Implantation what?" I felt as if I might start hyperventilating any moment. Was she right? Was I pregnant? Had Ben knocked me up on our first night together?

"Some women have it really early in their pregnancy. It's when the egg implants in your uterus. You bleed a little. It can happen around the same time you expect your period."

"Oh my God," I groaned, rubbing my face. Sore breasts. Nausea. Bloating. "Oh. My. God."

"Calm down," she urged, reaching over to grab my hand as she drove. "Listen, you're not in high school. You've got a degree. You've almost finished your MBA. You've got a job. You have a home. You're rich as fuck. You'll be fine. And, if you don't want to be a mom right now, you have options. Whatever decision you make, I'll support you."

"We make," I corrected, thinking of Ben. "If I'm pregnant, Ben has to be part of my decision."

"Definitely," she agreed, giving my hand a reassuring squeeze. "I'm sorry. I didn't mean to upset you."

"No, I'm glad you said something." Even though I was panicking, I truly was glad. "If I'm pregnant, I need to know sooner rather than later." A horrible thought struck me. "I've been drinking!"

"I'm sure it's fine. You're not a drunk."

"No, but I do have a glass of wine with dinner and we drank at brunch yesterday." Feeling like a monster, I looked down at my belly. Had I poisoned my baby? Had I doomed them before even knowing they existed?

"Aston, calm the fuck down," Marley ordered. "You are young, healthy and fit. Lots of women drink before they find out they're pregnant. It's going to be okay."

"I hope so," I whispered, disappointment and dread making my chest hurt. How could I not know? How had I ignored the signs?

"You're not calming down," Marley persisted. "You're going to have a panic attack, and I'm going to get yelled at by Ben."

"Ben wouldn't yell at you. He'd be too afraid Besian would punch him for it."

"Not funny," Marley said even though she laughed.

"He was at my house this morning."

"Ben?"

"Your Albanian admirer."

"Oh." She pretended to not be interested. "And?"

"It's a long story."

She looked at all the cars surrounding us. "We're stuck in traffic so…"

Wanting to think about anything except the possibility I might be pregnant, I told her everything. I started with Detective Dawson visiting me at work and didn't finish until I reached Besian's visit that morning. When I was done, I waited for her to say something.

"Holy shit," Marley remarked. "What a mess!" She bit her lower lip. "Do you think Margie and her baby are safe?"

"I hope so."

"Are we assholes for not calling the cops right now? To tell them that she and the baby aren't safe?"

"If we do, Ben will know it was me." I wrestled with the morality of it. "I don't want her or the baby to get hurt."

"Too late for that," Marley said as she turned into the Target shopping center. "Her husband put her and the baby at risk the second he started his illegal bullshit. Honestly, I'm surprised they haven't been hurt yet. He's obviously having some sort of money issues. That probably means he owes his Chinese counterparts. I don't know a lot about them, but I would imagine they wouldn't blink at offing a woman and her kid to send a message."

"I hope you're wrong."

"I hope she was taken by the FBI yesterday. That's the best thing that could happen to her and the baby." Marley maneuvered through the packed parking lot and eventually found an empty space along the side of the store. She put her Prius in park and sat behind the wheel as if thinking. Finally, she said, "Get the phone out of my glove box."

I did as she asked and handed it over. "What are you doing?"

"The right thing," she said, her voice full of reluctance. "We'll never be able to live with ourselves if something happens to her or the baby."

Even though I could have stopped her, I sat silently as she powered up the cheap burner and dialed 9-1-1. My stomach was in knots as she waited for the dispatcher to answer. Would Ben find out? Would he be furious? Would he get in trouble? How bad would his punishment be? I thought of the stories I had read of chopped off fingers and grimaced. *I'm sorry, Ben.*

"Hi, um, I have a tip about a woman and her baby who are in serious danger. Her name is Margie Metcalfe. She has a young baby. Her husband is Gary Metcalfe. He's involved in some shady money shit. The FBI raided their house yesterday morning. Her husband's enemies are planning to kidnap her and the baby. Please protect them."

Before the dispatcher could ask any questions, Marley ended the call and powered down the phone. She removed the battery and SIM card. Handing me the SIM card, she said, "When we get inside, go to the bathroom, wrap this in toilet paper and flush it. I'm going to dump these in the recycling bins up front."

"Okay."

"Do you keep burners?"

I shook my head. "Should I?"

"Yes."

"Then I guess we should put that on our shopping list," I remarked dryly.

"Not here," she disagreed. "They would be easy to trace back to you. We'll get some cash and go to a couple of different gas stations. You should keep a mix of different brands and carriers. Never pay with your card. Always cash. Don't buy more than one at a time."

"Right," I said, committing her lesson to memory.

Marley touched my hand and held my gaze. "If anyone finds out about the 9-1-1 call, you tell them it was me. I'm not afraid to go toe to toe with any of them. Spider will never let anyone hurt me."

"Jesus, Marley." I closed my eyes and wondered what the hell my life had become. "Am I doing the right thing?"

She shrugged. "It's not my business to tell you how to live your life. You can't help who you love. In the end, you have to decide what you can accept and what you can't."

Neither of us mentioned the possible baby complication. If I was pregnant, if I had a baby with Ben, even if I someday decided I couldn't take the crime family connection, I would never be able to break free. He would always be in our child's life—and so would his illicit activities.

Marley squeezed my hand. "We'll figure it out, Aston. We always do. You're not alone, okay? No matter what happens. We'll always have each other."

Feeling emotional, I hugged her tight. "You're the best bitch ever."

She laughed and hugged me back. "You're the best sister from another mister."

After we hugged it out, we got out of the car and headed into the store. Instead of sidestepping the empty carts left on the sidewalk by inconsiderate shoppers, we grabbed two of them and pushed them inside. I did as Marley had instructed, seguing into the bathroom to dispose of the SIM card before rejoining her at the Dollar Spot.

Our longstanding Sunday Target date wasn't as fun as usual. We were more subdued as we pushed our carts through the Dollar Spot and then through the clothing and beauty aisles. We spent almost ten minutes trying to figure out which pregnancy test was the best and finally decided to get one of each—a digital and one with two pink lines—and a bottle of prenatal gummy vitamins.

Eventually, we wandered into the home goods sections and hunted the end caps for bargains and clearance. My gaze wandered away from the soft throw blankets on clearance to the baby section. Seeing the baby gear made my heart do a weird little flip. I had always wanted to be a mom someday. It had always seemed like something I would do after I turned thirty, but now, here I was, twenty-four and facing the very real likelihood that my plans had drastically changed.

Unable to help myself, I pushed my cart toward the baby aisles. My hand glided over the smooth gray rail of a crib before testing the firmness of a crib mattress next to it. I stared at all of the different pieces of gear on display. Bouncers, swings, high chairs, exersaucers, walkers, strollers… My head was spinning by the time I reached the end of the aisle. Who knew babies needed so many things?

When I turned down the car seat aisle, I gawked at all of the straps and latches. They looked like the sort of thing an astronaut would ride in on a trip to Mars, not a seat for a baby. Some of them were part of travel systems—whatever the hell that was—and others seemed to be made for bigger kids. How long did a kid have to sit in one of those things?

The next aisle wasn't any more reassuring. There were shelves of formula from at least seven different brands, each one offering multiple options. Milk based. Soy based. Powder. Premade. Organic. Non-GMO. Sensitive. Professional. Advanced. For gassiness. For spit-up. For neuro support. For colic. Hypoallergenic.

Across the aisle, there were breast pumps and breastfeeding gear. I looked at one of the pumps on display and cringed. It looked like a torture device. It took me back to a dairy field trip I had taken as a kid. I remembered watching the farmer hook those huge silver milking tubes onto the cow's teats. Holding the human version made my stomach roll. How bad was that going to hurt?

That thought spurred worries of childbirth. I couldn't even imagine what kind of hell that was. I would definitely be one of the moms who got pain relief the second I stepped into the hospital. I didn't want to feel anything. I wanted to be blissfully unaware of my body being stretched to the breaking point.

As I left the formula aisle, I ended up in the section lined with layettes. I had bought baby clothes for friends or coworkers a few times. I had always just grabbed something ridiculously cute and called it a day. Standing here now, surrounded by pinks, blues, pale greens and sunny yellows, I felt an overwhelming urge to touch the soft fabrics. The newborn outfits were impossibly small. The socks were adorable, and the shoes were the sweetest little things I had ever seen.

"You okay?" Marley asked gently. She had obviously seen me going into the baby section, but she hadn't followed at first. She must have known I needed some space.

"Yeah," I said, voice thick with emotion. My eyes started to prickle with heat, and I blinked back tears I wasn't ready to shed. Inhaling a deep, steadying breath, I said, "I think I'm ready to go."

"Okay. Sure."

Grateful for Marley's friendship, I followed her to the front of the store and picked a short line. She moved through the checkout line next to mine and finished a few minutes before me. When we met up again, we piled our bags into my cart and gave hers to an employee straightening them out by the entrance.

"You're going to be a great mom," Marley said as we neared her car. "Whether that's sometime later this year or in a decade," she clarified. "You will be an amazing mother."

"How can you know that?" I asked, fearful that I would end up just like my mother.

"Because you're an amazing friend," she answered as if it were the most obvious thing in the world. "You're selfless, caring and kind. You're generous. You love with your whole heart. You do the right thing even when it sucks." She unlocked the trunk so we could load our bags. "Deep down inside, you know that you told me about Margie and her baby because you were worried about them. You knew I wouldn't be able to let it go. You couldn't make the call yourself because you were conflicted about betraying Ben, but you made sure I would. You did the right thing, even if it was hard."

She was right, of course. She was always right. She could see through me and read me better than anyone, maybe even better than Ben.

Not sure what to say and deciding I didn't need to say anything because she had already said it best, I took hold of the cart. "I'll take this back."

"Sure."

As she closed the trunk, I turned around with the cart and pushed it across the parking lot to the closest cart corral. On my walk back to her car, I paused to let an SUV pass. I hadn't noticed the minivan next to us before, but I could see there was someone sitting in the middle row. The van was really close to the passenger door, and I hoped I wouldn't bump it when I tried to get into my seat.

Before I had even touched the handle of my door, the sliding door of the idling minivan opened quickly behind me. Startled, I turned to see who it was, but I wasn't fast enough. A heartbeat later, a man had his arm across the front of my throat. He pressed his face to my ear and hissed, "You scream. I'll kill you."

Certain he was going to kill me anyway, I fucking screamed. I screamed like a virgin in a horror film running from a machete wielding psycho at a summer camp.

He swore angrily and jammed something hard under my shirt and into the sensitive skin of my underarm. A second later, a painful shock stole my breath. I gasped and jerked as the electricity rocketed through my body. Gripped with intense pain, I sagged in his arms as my vision tunneled to black.

Marley screamed, and her voice faded into nothing along with my consciousness.

CHAPTER THIRTEEN

WITH NOTHING HELPFUL to report, Ben strode into the club, careful to avoid the power cords and construction equipment in his path. The boss's newest acquisition had been undergoing renovations for almost a month, including the parking lot. What had been an ugly eyesore on the corner of a busy street was now hidden behind tall evergreens that would shield the patrons from prying eyes and appease the neighboring business owners who weren't thrilled to have a topless joint right across the street or next door.

He crossed the floor, edging along the newly revamped main stage and then following the line of the bar top to the door that led to the back of house. There were a few familiar faces in the hallway, and he nodded at them before stopping outside Besian's office. He rapped his knuckles against the door and waited.

"Come in."

He stepped inside the office and shut the door behind him. Besian removed his reading glasses, setting them aside and out of the way as if embarrassed that he needed them. He closed the folder in front of him and leaned back in his chair. "Well?"

"Nothing." Ben dropped into the chair across from the boss. "Not even the Russians have been able to find them."

Besian swore in Albanian before he rubbed his face and sighed. "I'm waiting for Kostya. He was checking in with one of his little spiders. He thinks the FBI probably picked up the wife and baby."

Trying to set him at ease, Ben said, "Is it really that bad for us? We're not involved in whatever the hell Gary, Paul and Calvin were doing. We were victims in their crimes."

"That won't stop the police from dragging us all in and sweating us," Besian replied. His hand moved to his chest, touching the spot where he had been shot. Was he in pain? Had it become a nervous tic to touch it? To remind himself he was alive?

"No, it won't," Ben agreed.

The door opened suddenly, and Ben jumped to his feet, instinctively moving in front of Besian. It was only Kostya, but Ben didn't relax. It was impossible to feel at ease around the infamous Russian cleaner. Ben had witnessed Kostya working on a guy once, and the experience had left him violently shaking and sick. Just the smell of leather or the sound of metal clanging against metal would take him right back to that night in a soundproofed storage building. Until then, he had never realized how much a man could bleed without dying.

Slamming the door behind him, Kostya stormed across the room. "You have a fucking problem."

"Tell me something I don't know," Besian replied dryly.

"This." Kostya held up his phone and tapped the screen.

"Hi, um, I have a tip about a woman and her baby who are in serious danger. Her name is Margie Metcalfe. She has a young baby. Her husband is Gary Metcalfe. He's involved in some shady money shit. The FBI raided their house yesterday morning. Her husband's enemies are planning to kidnap her and the baby. Please protect them."

Ben slanted a stealthy glance toward Besian who had clearly recognized the voice just as he had. *Marley.* He bit back the growl of frustration that threatened to erupt. She could have only gotten that information from Aston. *She betrayed us.*

He couldn't blame her for trying to help her coworker. She had known Margie much longer than she had known him, after all. The woman had a baby and was innocent in all the shit her husband done. Aston had a soft heart and telling Marley was something he should have anticipated. He hadn't thought it needed to be said. He had been certain she understood that was a secret she needed to keep.

"Why is your girlfriend calling 9-1-1, Ben?" Kostya pinned him with a furious glare.

"It's not Aston," Besian corrected roughly. He sat forward in his chair. "It's Marley."

"Oh, that's fucking great," Kostya snarled. "Now, we have two of them running their mouths?"

"Easy," Ben warned, not in the mood to hear the cleaner going after Aston or Marley.

"Easy? What the hell were you thinking telling your girlfriend about our plan?"

"He didn't," Besian interjected. "I told her."

"Have you lost your fucking mind?" Kostya reacted with shock and anger.

"No, but you have if you think you can come into my office and talk to me like that," Besian snarled, his usually contained temper flaring dangerously.

Kostya clenched his jaw and turned his attention to Ben.

"You need to get your girl under control—or else."

Ben bristled. "Are you threatening her?"

"If it means she'll get in line and do what she's told? Fucking yes."

"Hey, hey, hey," Besian said, jumping up from his chair and rushing to step between them. "Cut it out. Both of you. We are not going to brawl in my office."

Before Ben could protest, a scuffle in the hallway gained his attention. Besian and Kostya heard it, too. Shoulder to shoulder, they turned toward the door and the raised voices of the guards. They were trying to prevent someone from coming into the office, but another voice shouted, "Houston PD, open up!"

Kostya let loose a streak of Russian, each phrase nastier than the last. Wordlessly, Besian strode to the door and yanked it open. Not even bothering to fake politeness, he asked, "Santos, what the fuck do you want?"

"Him." Eric pointed at Ben.

"Me?"

"Why?" Besian demanded.

"Have you heard from Aston in the last couple of hours?" Eric asked, ignoring Besian's query.

"No." He reached for his back pocket and retrieved his phone. There weren't any messages from her. "She and Marley were headed out to Target. They go every Sunday. It's their thing."

Eric's usual hardass expression softened. "I'm sorry, Ben, but I have to show you something that's going to upset you."

Fear gripped his heart. Out of the corner of his eye, he could see Besian and Kostya exchange concerned glances. Like him, they knew that Eric wouldn't apologize or try to be nice unless he had earth shattering news to share.

Eric turned his phone toward Ben. "We had a bunch of 9-1-1 calls coming from a Target parking lot. This is what we found on the security feeds."

Ben's heart raced, and he swallowed anxiously as Eric tapped the play triangle on his phone screen. At first, Ben didn't notice anything unusual. It was almost a minute before Marley and Aston came into view with their Target cart. They seemed to be talking about something serious, maybe that phone call Marley had made earlier. They placed their bags in the trunk, and Aston pushed the cart to the corral while Marley got behind the wheel and started her car.

On her way back to the car, Aston seemed to turn her attention to the minivan idling in the space next to theirs. He couldn't tell from the camera's angle, but he thought there was someone in the middle row of seats. Just as that thought registered, the passenger door suddenly slid open and a man leapt out and grabbed Aston. She struggled and screamed.

Her attacker had something in his right hand. A gun? Aston screamed again and jerked wildly, as if being electrocuted. A stun gun? A Taser? She dropped like a sack of rocks, and her assailant threw her into the van, shoving her legs out of the way so he could close the door.

Like a wild hellion, Marley launched herself over the hood of her car and started wailing on the man who had hurt Aston. Kicking and scratching and slapping, she beat the hell out of him. The man reared back with his fist and slammed it right into her face. Ben winced as Marley flew back into the car, her face instantly bloodied. It was a horrific hit. She was a small woman, and the attacker was his size, strong enough to break her jaw if he had tapped her in just the right place.

The attacker snatched Marley up and jammed the device he held into her neck. She didn't have much of a fight left in her, and she went down quickly. Blood poured from her face as the man picked her up and threw her into the van on top of Aston. He glanced around the parking lot and seemed to notice the small crowd watching and yelling. From the back of his pants, he pulled a gun and fired it into the air, dispersing the crowd. He got behind the wheel and raced out of the parking lot, disappearing from the camera's view.

Fury raged through Ben like a wildfire. His fists curled at his sides, and he fought the urge to punch the nearest wall. He wanted to destroy the man who had dared to hurt Aston.

"We think it was Gary Metcalfe that grabbed them," Eric said finally. He tucked his phone into the pocket of his thin jacket. "His wife and baby went missing last night. Before you ask," he held up a hand, "it wasn't us or the Feds. I've already been to see Nikolai who assured me that none of you had them."

"We don't," Besian confirmed.

"You sure? Because it's a strange coincidence that a 9-1-1 call came from a tower right near that Target warning that someone wanted to grab Gary's wife and baby," Eric said with narrowed eyes. "An hour later, Aston and Marley are grabbed from that same parking lot by Gary? I mean, come on."

"You calling me a liar?" Besian asked.

"Wouldn't be the first time," Eric replied.

Besian scoffed and shook his head. "We don't have them. Period. End of fucking story. If we did, I would be on the phone right now trading them for Aston and Marley."

"So, who has them?" Eric asked, clearly out of his depth now. "We have nothing. No leads. Unless you know something that can help us, I don't have a good feeling about the girls making it through the night."

Hearing the detective assess the situation that way was like a punch to the gut. Ben's anger disappeared as he felt like puking. Eric was right. If Gary had taken Aston and Marley to try to get his wife and baby back, it wasn't going to work. The people who had his family would leave no loose ends. They would kill all five of them and be done with it.

As if having the same thought, Besian met his gaze. They shared a look that communicated what they were both thinking. *We have to get the fuck out of here and shake any police that follow us.*

"There's something else, Ben." Reluctantly, he said, "We searched Marley's car. One of the bags had two pregnancy tests in it and a bottle of prenatal vitamins."

Staggered by the information, Ben couldn't hear anything but the pounding of blood against his eardrums. *Pregnant?*

At any other time, he would have taken the news of a possible baby with Aston as something to smile about and enjoy. Now, though, it added an even worse layer of terror. He didn't even want to think about what a stun gun could do to a tiny little baby. Would she miscarry? Alone? Tied up in the dark?

"We don't know which one of them bought them," Eric continued.

"Marley isn't seeing anyone right now," he answered. "It had to be Aston."

Besian placed a steadying hand on his shoulder. He spoke

to him in Albanian, his voice low as he promised, "Stay calm. We'll find them—and then we'll kill that motherfucker."

"I'm not even going to ask you translate that," Eric said, raising his hands. "Since I can tell you aren't going to cooperate, I'm out of here. I said what I came to say. We'll be working the case. If you learn anything that might be helpful and you want to share, you know how to find me."

"*Ne 36 gusht*," Besian muttered.

Ben's mouth curved with the ghost of a smile at that. *On August 36.* In other words, fucking never.

Eric hesitated in the doorway. "I hope you find her, Ben."

After he was gone, Ben wondered if he really did. As if reading his mind, Kostya said, "He lost a girl he loved. He's been an asshole ever since."

Ben eyed Besian as he walked to his desk and opened the top drawer. He withdrew a shoulder holster and the two Berettas he preferred. This was the second time someone had kidnapped Marley in less than a year. The first time, Besian had taken a bullet to the chest to protect her. Ben hoped like hell they weren't about to repeat history.

"Let's go." Besian strode by them and out the door.

"Where?" Ben asked, looking to Kostya for guidance. If anyone had an idea where to start their search, he would.

Kostya ignored him and lifted his phone to his ear. Ben trailed the cleaner as he left the office. "It's me. I need the list of properties you were working on earlier. Call me when you have it."

Without an invitation, Kostya slid into the front passenger seat of Besian's waiting car. Ben took a spot in the back. He hated feeling out of control and unable to help. He swallowed the pain threatening to overwhelm him.

Kostya was on the phone again. He spoke hurriedly in Russian, and Ben only managed to understand a handful of the words. He seemed to be telling Nikolai about the kidnapping of Aston and Marley. When he hung up, he said, "Anything you need, he'll give."

The cleaner's phone chimed, and he swiped his finger across the screen. He rattled off an address. "Let's try there first."

Ben closed his eyes and cursed silently. This was going to take forever.

What if Aston doesn't have that much time?

CHAPTER FOURTEEN

"**I** AM GETTING really fucking tired of this," Marley grumbled from somewhere behind me. "Psycho criminal assholes kidnapping me and tying me up," she muttered. "I hate this damn town."

As I came to on the hard, cheaply carpeted floor, I blinked rapidly. My stomach lurched, and I barely had enough time to turn my head before a rush of vomit escaped.

"Aston! Shit. Hang on." After a bit of huffing and scooting, Marley got close enough to help me. She used her bound wrists to hold my head as I wretched. "Hey! Asshole! We need help!"

None other than Gary Metcalfe appeared in the doorway of what appeared to be an empty office. His panicked gaze dropped to the pile of mess I had made.

"Don't just stand there!" Marley snapped angrily. "She's pregnant. She needs some water and a towel or something."

"Pregnant?" he repeated, horrified.

"Did I stutter?" Marley yelled. "Get us some water!"

He snapped to and ran from the room, hopefully to find the water Marley had ordered. My throat was on fire, and a terrible taste clung to my mouth. With Marley's help, I managed to sit up despite the plastic ties on my wrists and ankles. My gaze finally traveled to her face, and I gasped. "Marley! Your face!"

"It looks worse than it is," she assured me. "I don't think anything is broken."

"Are you sure?"

She nodded. "I touched all the sore spots. My bones feel normal."

Glaring at the empty doorway, I swore, "I'm going to kill him."

"Not if I get to him first," she said under her breath.

Noticing the sheen of sweat and the strange pallor to her skin, I asked, "Are you feeling okay?"

"Just kind of anxious feeling," she said, waving me off. "It's nothing."

"It doesn't look like nothing."

"It's fine. It's probably just low blood sugar or something. We got electrocuted by that psycho. I'm sure that burned through our energy reserves."

She was trying to keep me calm by downplaying her situation, but I sensed there was more to it than just low blood sugar.

"I'm sorry, Marley." Unable to control my emotions, I started crying. Not quietly either. Big, ugly, loud sobs. "I'm sorry. This is all my fault."

"Hey, no," she soothed. "This isn't your fault. It's not my fault. It's not even Ben's fault. This is the fault of greedy, stupid men."

"She's right," Gary said as he cautiously entered the room where he had stowed us. He had a paper cup with water in one hand and some wet paper towels in the other. "We were greedy and stupid." He gently tipped the cup to my mouth. "Here. Drink."

Grateful for the water, I gulped it down. He carefully wiped my face and then dragged me into a more comfortable position leaning against a wall. For a moment, I considered hitting him with my fists, but I couldn't possibly get up fast enough to run. I had no idea where we were or if we could even get help. For now, it was safer to sit here.

Marley wasn't nearly as cooperative as he tried to help her sit next to me. She insulted and kicked at him, but he didn't stop trying and eventually got her leaned against the wall.

"I know you two won't believe me," he said, stepping back from us, "but I don't want to hurt you. That's not the plan."

"What is the plan?" I asked, wondering what the hell he was trying to accomplish by kidnapping us. "You have to know that there are people looking for us. I'm sure someone called 9-1-1 at Target, and I know that Ben is going to lose it when he realizes I'm missing."

"Spider will have the entire club searching the city for me," Marley added. "You're so screwed, man."

"I was screwed before I grabbed you two." Gary snatched the only chair in the room and sank down on it. Head hung low, he sighed and scrubbed his fingers through his hair. "They took Margie and Elliot."

Marley and I exchanged glances before I asked, "Who took them?"

"Triad," he said and roughly wiped his face. "It was never supposed to go like this. It was just a chance to make some extra money. Margie was climbing higher and higher, bringing in more money and bagging more promotions, and I was stagnant. She said she didn't care, but I was too dumb to believe her. She didn't care. At all. It was never about money for her."

His ramblings weren't meant for us. He seemed to be confessing all his transgressions as if desperate to clean himself of the mistakes he had made.

"Were you laundering money?" I asked, deciding I wanted to know the truth—whatever it was. "Did Calvin rope you into it?"

"Yeah." Gary sat back in his chair. "He had used my company to hold some money when he liquidated the assets he inherited from his mother. He seemed a bit off, but I chalked it up to being raised with money and let it go. When he approached me three years ago with this money laundering scheme, I said no. I didn't want any part of it. I was proud of the business I had built."

"But?" Marley asked.

"But I couldn't stop thinking about the potential for profit," he admitted. "I saw dollar signs and ignored the risk. I accepted his offer, and he introduced me to Paul Chen. Paul was the connection between the Triad and Calvin. There were a couple of real estate agents we used for the transactions. They're all connected to the Triad through family back in China. We sat down and figured out how the scheme would function and got to work for the Chinese mafia."

"Selling and buying commercial real estate through LLC's and cutouts," I clarified.

"Yeah. It was simple. Nothing tricky or fancy. It was easy, under the radar shit. We had layers of shell companies between the money coming from China, my company and the clean money flowing into US banks. It was perfect."

"Until?" Marley wondered.

"Until that crazy fucker decided he was going to be some big-time drug kingpin," Greg snarled. "He kept talking about moving in on cartel territory and cutting them out of the Houston drug business. He wanted to be the funnel for Asian narcotics. Crazy bastard," he muttered. "He had so many grand ideas, but he was shit at the follow through. After he disappeared, Paul and I were fucked," Gary continued. "We looked everywhere for him. We think he was probably offed by the cartel for trying to shove into their territory."

"Probably," I agreed, assiduously ignoring Marley's glances.

"Once he was gone, we realized the paranoid asshole had moved money owed to the Chinese into accounts only he could access. The Triad didn't give a shit. They wanted their payouts."

Suddenly, it made sense to me. "So, you started siphoning legit client funds to pay the mafia?"

"Exactly," Gary said. "I didn't have a choice. These guys are brutal. I thought I could just float the funds until we could get access to those accounts."

"But you got caught," Marley guessed.

Gary nodded. "Some of my legitimate clients needed funds to buy properties, and I didn't have it. I tried to dodge them, but that only lasts so long. By the time Margie told me that the Feds were questioning her at work, I knew it was over. At that point, I had to make a decision. The only thing that mattered to me was keeping Margie and Elliot safe."

"By robbing the Albanians? And that other gang?"

He shook his head. "You don't understand. I needed the money. I had to make my payments or else they were going to kill us. I had to keep my family safe."

"They would have been safer with the FBI," Marley interjected as if he were the stupidest man she had ever met. "Why didn't you just drive straight to the police department and turn yourself in and ask for help protecting your family?"

"Obviously, I'm a fucking idiot who doesn't think clearly when I'm stressed," Gary shouted angrily. "I'm a fuck up, okay? I panicked."

"No," Marley countered, "you didn't panic. You're a coward. You decided to risk your wife and your baby rather than man up and admit your crimes to the police. You're afraid of prison. You ran like a little bitch, playing all these convoluted games, and now your wife and baby are probably going to die."

Shocked into silence by her outburst, Gary looked ashen and shaken. It must have been hard to hear the truth. It must have been difficult to swallow that he had failed to protect his family.

Worried that Marley may have pushed him too far, I gently asked, "How much money do you need to get square with the Triad?"

His gaze whipped to my face. "What?"

"How much do you need?"

"Millions."

"Like five or fifty?" I asked, exasperated. "It matters."

"Thirteen point six."

"Okay." I searched my brain for the easiest way to get my hands on that kind of money even though I had absolutely no intention to follow through with it. "It's Sunday, and I won't be able to access to funds until tomorrow. I would have to structure it in a way that we don't run afoul of the IRS. I don't need trouble like that."

"You cannot be serious," Marley interrupted. "You are not giving this asshole money."

"No, I'm not giving him money," I agreed, hoping she would continue arguing with me to make my offer seem real. "I'm going to give it to the Triad, but only after they release Margie and the baby."

"They'll just come back for more," Marley argued. "You cannot deal with these people. They're criminals. Once you start feeding them cash, they will never stop asking for more."

"So, I'm just supposed to let Margie and the baby die?" I hissed angrily. "What do you expect me to do, Marley?"

"Not this," she ground out. "You can't do this."

"I can do whatever the hell I want with my money."

"You're making a mistake," she insisted. "You'll regret this, Aston."

"Probably," I agreed.

Pursing her lips, Marley blew out a noisy breath and refused to look at me. I turned my attention back to Gary who seemed stunned by my offer. "Do you have a way to contact them?"

He nodded. "They aren't very open to negotiation."

"You haven't ever heard me negotiate."

He hesitated and then stood up, reaching into his pocket and retrieving a pocket knife. I held my breath as he knelt in front of me and cut the ties binding my wrists and ankles. Finally able to move, I stretched my cramping neck and shoulders. When he knelt in front of Marley, Gary seemed reluctant to release her. I didn't blame him. She was probably going to wallop him for what he had done to her face.

"You kick me or hit me, and I'm going to stab you," he warned.

She rolled her eyes. "Whatever, tough guy."

He scowled at her as he cut the ties and hurried to get out range. Pocket knife still in hand, he waited to see if Marley was going to make a go of it. When she stayed next to me, he relaxed a bit. "I'm going to get one of the burners I brought. I'll be right back."

Clearly not trusting us to stay put, he locked the door from the outside, caging us inside. Marley pushed off the floor and stood. Reaching down, she helped me to my feet. I felt woozy, and she stepped into me, bracing my body with her own. "You okay?"

"Just dizzy," I said with a nonchalant wave of my hand. "I'll be fine."

"You need to see a doctor."

"So do you," I replied, noting her terribly battered face and her shaking hands.

"I'm not the one who is knocked up."

"I may not be either."

She shot me a *really* look. "So," she sighed, "what's the plan? Because I know you aren't crazy enough to give money to the Triad."

"I couldn't think of a better way to get him to believe we're on his side."

"It worked."

"Do you know where we are? Did you see how we got in

here or how to get out?"

"We're on the third floor," she said with certainty. "You were passed out when we got here so he perp-walked me up here. We used the elevators. He locked me in here. He went back out to get you. I think we could find our way out. We should probably stick to the stairs."

"And then what?"

"If we can knock him down or out, we can steal his keys and phone and make a run for it."

"And if we can't? If he really does stab one of us?"

"He won't stab you," she said, sounding a bit breathless. She seemed to be sweating again, and my concern skyrocketed. "You have access to the money he needs."

"I don't want him to stab you!"

"Then we better not let him get away from us if we decide to attack him," she said decisively. "Go watch the window. Let me know when he's coming."

"Okay."

She glanced around the room as if searching for makeshift weapons. "The chair is too bulky to throw or swing." She hurried to the desk and started rifling through the drawers. "Jackpot!" She produced a letter opener and a pair of scissors and slashed them through the air. "Now whose about to get stabbed?"

"You are really scary sometimes." I stared at her in a new light. "Like really scary." Movement outside caught my attention. Lowering my voice, I hissed, "He's coming!"

"Here." She pressed the scissors into my hand. "Go for his soft spots—eyes, neck, belly. Just fuck him up."

"When this is over, you need therapy," I whispered as

Gary unlocked the door. "Like, seriously, get some help."

The door opened before she could make a smartass remark. In a flash, she was on him. He howled as the letter opener slid deep into his forearm as he tried to block her attack. She screamed and ripped it free before trying to get him again. He stumbled back into the hallway, and she followed and slashed his chest, gouging a nasty wound. Not ready to go down without a fight, he kicked out at her and connected with her belly. With a loud *oof,* Marley fell back into the wall.

Watching my friend get kicked was too much. I lost it. I ran at him, scissors raised and ready to strike. Just as I sank the scissors into the soft area under his shoulder, an elevator dinged somewhere nearby. We all froze. Marley halfway standing. Me with the tip of the scissors embedded in his skin. Gary flinching in pain. The ding was followed by men shouting in Cantonese. I suddenly regretted not paying better attention in the Chinese lessons my father had insisted I take for so many years.

Marley and I glanced at each other. She grabbed my hand, hers feeling cold and clammy against mine. "We have to go. Now!"

I looked back at Gary, but Marley tugged hard. "Now, Aston!"

We raced through the maze of hallways, slamming into the walls as we rounded corners. When we made it to the stairwell, we locked the doors behind us, trying to slow down any pursuers. Marley led the way, her feet moving quickly despite the physical blows she had taken. I wobbled a bit, my head spinning and my stomach rolling with nausea.

A gunshot cracked, and we both gasped. We exchanged

panicked looks. Our survival instincts kicked into overdrive. We ran faster, taking the stairs two at a time before we reached the bottom floor and a long hallway. Finally—*finally*—we spotted a set of double doors that led outside.

"Shit!" Marley jerked on the door handles, but they wouldn't budge. "They're locked from outside."

"Oh, come on!" I pounded my fists against the door, not believing that it was going to end like this. "Fuck!"

"Wait. Hold on!" Marley grabbed my hand and pulled me close. "I see something."

On tiptoes, she looked through the rectangular window on the upper part of the door. "It's people. Men," she clarified. "Shit. *Shit.*"

"Is it them? The Triad?" I gripped her hand so tightly my fingers started to go numb.

"I can't tell. It's gotten dark outside. They're coming closer," she whispered, her voice filled with dread. "I can't tell if— *wait.* Wait! Oh my God!" She started slapping her hand against the door, her sweaty palms leaving prints on the metal. "Besian! Besian!"

"What?" I pushed in closer and looked through the other window. My heart fluttered in my chest when I saw the man next to Besian and rushing toward the door. "Ben! Ben! Help!"

"It's locked!" Marley yelled as Besian tried the handle. "We can't get out! Please! You have to hurry! They shot Gary. They're coming for us!"

"Get back!" Ben ordered. "Step to the side, as far away as you can get."

We huddled against the far wall. Outside, the men were yelling. Inside the building and not far away, the sound of men running and opening doors echoed. We were trapped between the men who could save us and the men who wanted to kill us.

"Stay back!" Ben shouted again. "Cover your ears!"

I clapped my hands over my ears and closed my eyes. Two of the loudest shotgun blasts I had ever heard ripped through the hallway. Not in all of the times my dad had dragged me along dove hunting had I had ever heard anything like that. It was as if they had fired a cannon at the door, blowing the locks right out of the metal.

The doors were shoved open, and Ben and Besian rushed into the building. More men followed them, all of them armed to the teeth. Devil, Ben's scarred best friend, was among them. He had a wicked shotgun in hand, the barrel strangely shaped and obviously meant for breaching doors. I didn't even want to know why he had one of those handy.

Before Marley and I could untangle ourselves and stand, all of the men surrounded us and formed a human wall. On the other side of them, the squeal of shoes on linoleum echoed. Looking through the cracks between the men shielding us, I could see the Triad members who had shot Gary.

Marley clasped my hand, her fingers trembling. She leaned close and whispered, "The first gunshot, we run."

I wanted to argue and refuse to leave Ben behind, but I knew what he would say. He would tell me to run. To fight. To live.

My hand slid down to the still flat front of my belly. *For our baby.*

CHAPTER FIFTEEN

ADRENALINE SURGED THROUGH Ben's bloodstream. His hands clenched and unclenched at his sides. He had a hard time slowing his breaths as he faced the armed gang that had been chasing after Aston and Marley.

He didn't even want to think what might have happened if Kostya hadn't gotten the tip when he did. If Nikolai hadn't reached out to the old man in Moscow and if Maksim hadn't agreed to call his Chinese counterpart, they would never have found the girls in time. There were too many properties, too many possibilities and not enough time or men to search them all.

But they had made it in time. Aston looked okay, shaken and scared, but Marley looked terrible. The bruises and blood smeared on her face were bad, but she seemed out of breath and oddly pale. He hoped it was only from the running and fear.

Both women needed to see a doctor, but first, they had to negotiate their way out of here without a shootout.

"Where is Metcalfe?" Besian asked. "Is he dead?"

"If he's not, he will be soon," the man who seemed to be their leader answered. He spoke with a British accent and seemed to be very comfortable conversing in English. He held himself like a powerful, well-educated man, and he was young, maybe closer to Aston's age, which meant he was hungry to prove himself. He was definitely going to be trouble. "Gut shot."

Ben grimaced. That was a horrible way to go, the death slow and agonizing.

"Good," Besian coldly replied. "And his wife and baby?"

"Safe at a secure site."

"I've been instructed to ask you to release them."

The man scoffed. "I've been instructed to hold them until we get our money."

"Not the smartest play," Besian remarked. "You haven't even established a foothold in the city yet, and you've already gained the attention of the police and Feds. You kill a woman and her baby? You'll never do business here again."

"I can't go back without my money."

"Not my fucking problem," Besian gruffly replied. "That's why I don't do business with people I can't trust. You've learned an expensive mistake." He shrugged. "We all do at some point."

"So has Gary," the man countered. "His mistake cost him his life and the lives of his wife and baby."

"You cannot kill Margie and Elliot," Aston interjected forcefully, pushing her way to the front. Ben tried to stop her, but she shrugged off his hands and ignored his pointed glare.

Besian was not in the mood for her help. "Take Marley and go outside."

She ignored him, her gaze fixed on the lead Triad. "No."

Besian's eyes narrowed dangerously. If she were anyone else, he might have dragged her out kicking and screaming. He seemed to sense that arguing with her was a lost cause. That or he didn't want to make a scene that would further undermine his authority.

Not giving one shit about Besian's irritated scowl, Aston stepped forward and held out her hand. "I'm Aston McNeil."

"Teddy Leung," the leader said, grasping her hand and holding it far longer than necessary for a handshake. "I know quite a bit about you, Miss McNeil. I'm very glad to finally meet you in person."

Ben bristled, unable to discern from Teddy's tone whether he was flirting or threatening. Either way, he didn't like it.

"You have me at a disadvantage, then," she said, carefully removing her hand. "I'm afraid I'm not at all familiar with you."

"You will be," Teddy promised with a smile that made Ben want to punch him right in his perfect fucking teeth. "You know I followed your father's deal with CIC very closely. That was quite a feat he managed."

"Dad always told me that if you're not growing, you're dying," she explained. "He saw the sovereign wealth fund as an opportunity. So far, he was proven correct."

"And would you take a risk like that, Miss McNeil?"

"Yes. Without hesitation," she added. "Selling that small stake in our firm gave my father the capital injection he needed to found StrateCore."

Assuming Ben and the rest of them had no idea what she was talking about, Teddy decided to enlighten them. "Strate-Core is the European arm of the Limestone Group. They're valuing the company north of ten billion."

"It was Dad's last big deal, and I intend to see it through," she stated.

"I'm sure you'll make your father very proud," Teddy replied with a smile that made Ben's hands clench at his sides.

"Dad gave me the tools I need to succeed."

"It's a pity he wasn't able to give your brother those same tools," Teddy said. "We were assured that Calvin had been mentored at your father's side, but it seems that we were misled."

"Calvin had a nasty habit of lying. His whole life was nothing but a con. He wanted what my father had, but he didn't have the work ethic necessary for it."

"Yes, I've come to see that." Teddy studied her for a moment. "You're sure you have no idea where to find him?"

"None. I haven't seen him in weeks," she answered honestly. "He came to the house and demanded some paperwork from my dad's safe. I gave it to him, and he left."

That was the censored version of that night's events. The heavily censored version.

"I see."

Did he? Ben couldn't tell if Teddy Leung understood that Calvin was dead and not just missing. Surely, by now, he had come to the conclusion that someone had knocked off that evil shit.

"You understand what a difficult position your brother's disappearance has put me in, Aston," he said with a deceptively nice tone.

"I do."

"He stole from me. Do you think your man and his family walk away when someone steals from them?"

"No," she answered immediately. "I think they make a

statement, a very clear and very loud one."

"So why should I walk away with nothing?"

"You should walk away because you want to make *real* money," she said. "What you lost in this scheme is pocket change compared to what you could make legally. You keep pursuing this, and you're going to end up on the FBI's radar, if you're not there already. If the Feds were raiding Gary's house two days ago, they already have their hands on the missing money. They'll have seized all the funds within their jurisdiction. They're waiting for someone to try to access them so they can swoop in and arrest them. I know that's not what you want."

"It's not," he agreed.

"The people who stole from you are dead. Calvin is gone. No one has seen him in weeks. With the number of people he double-crossed, it was only a matter of time before someone killed him," she said. "Gary is upstairs dying. Paul Chen is on ice in a morgue somewhere. It's done," she said with a slash of her hand. "Let Margie and the baby go. You'll only find more trouble if you don't. That's not a smart way to do business."

Teddy considered her words. "And what about my lost money?"

"That's the risk of the free market."

"If we're talking free market, you should know I can recoup some of my lost money by selling your friend and her baby."

Ben stiffened at the disgusting threat.

"And how much do a woman and a baby go for on the free market?" Aston asked without missing a beat.

"For you?" Teddy grinned lasciviously. "Let's say, oh, forty percent of what I'm owed? I'm sure Gary apprised you of the amount."

"He did."

"And?"

"It depends on how you want the funds."

Ben glanced between Aston and Teddy. He wanted to grab her and ask her what the hell she was thinking. She couldn't seriously be considering buying her friend and baby from the Chinese mafia!

"I suspect cash would be a bit difficult," Teddy said. "Can you get your hands on crypto?"

She nodded. "If that's your preference."

"It is."

"I will need a few days to get that much together."

"A week?" he offered.

"A week," she agreed.

"Until then, I'll need to hold some collateral. I'm sure you understand."

"Such as?"

"I'm told you have a very nice house and that your father had quite an art collection."

"Had being the operative word," she clarified. "He gave away almost all of the art or sent it to museums in the name of our family trust. The house, however…"

"I'm listening, Miss McNeil."

"You can have the house as collateral on the crypto. If I don't come through in seven days, it's yours. Deal?"

Teddy considered her offer and nodded. "I like the way you do business, Miss McNeil." He held out his hand. "I think we're going to be very successful together."

It took everything Ben had not to wrench Teddy's hand away from hers. Even if it was hypocritical, he didn't want the filth of the criminal world touching her.

Teddy looked at one of his lackeys and barked an order in Chinese. The man took out his phone and made a quick call. When his goon was finished, Teddy smiled at Aston. "Your friend and her baby are being released in the parking lot of the nearest police station."

"Thank you, Teddy."

"You're very welcome, Aston. I'll be in touch. Perhaps we can have lunch next week to finish our little deal?"

"I'll check my calendar," she replied coolly.

Teddy laughed, and with a snap of his fingers, he wordlessly ordered his men to follow him out of the building.

When they were out of sight, Ben grabbed Aston and whirled her around to face him. "What the hell are you doing?"

"The right thing," she answered, her chin lifted high and daring him to argue.

"They're the Chinese Mafia!"

"And you're the Albanian mafia," she stated calmly. "I'm part of this world—your world—forever. There is no point in trying to run from it. It's the choice we've both made."

Ben stared at her for a long moment. Not caring that he was surrounded by men who would rag him to hell and back later, he cupped her face and kissed her. For better or worse, she had chosen him. She had chosen to tie herself to him, and he was determined to make sure she would never regret it. "I love you, Aston."

"You better," she murmured against his mouth. "Or else

I'm going to set Marley on your ass. She took out Gary with a letter opener."

Ben glanced at her best friend in shock. "A letter opener?"

Looking less pale and breathing more normally, Marley shrugged as she gingerly prodded her swollen mouth. "It's all I could find. She jammed a pair of scissors into his chest."

Ben turned to Aston with an approving smile. "Good for you."

"I hate to break this up, but you need to leave," Kostya interrupted. "I'll keep the girls here and make sure the site is clean. I'll call the police when it's safe."

Reluctant to go but certain it had to be this way, Ben kissed her one last time. She waved him off, urging him to go before the police arrived, and he did.

The boss fell into step beside him and stayed silent for the entire drive to the club they had left earlier. Sitting in the parking lot, Ben held his phone and waited for it to ring. He grew more agitated with each passing moment. How much longer would this take?

"Aston needs to be reminded of her place."

"She seems to be fully aware of her place in my life," Ben replied, not at all in the mood for one of Besian's lectures.

Besian scowled at him "You know what I mean."

"I meant what I said," Ben answered forcefully. "She's never going to be the woman you expect her to be. She's not going to stay behind, out of the loop and uninformed. She's not that girl—and I don't want her to be."

"Then you need to marry her," Besian spoke finally. "She's clearly decided you're worth the trouble. Lock that shit down now."

Ben had assumed that someday he would ask Aston to marry him. Someday in the future. The far future. When she was done with her MBA. When his shop was turning steady profits. When he had extricated himself as far as possible from the clutches of the family business.

"You can't wait," Besian continued, as if reading his mind. "You can't testify against each other if you're married. That stunt she pulled with Leung is proof enough that you both need that protection."

"I'm not going to ask her to marry me for legal coverage."

"Then ask her because she's having your baby."

Ben swallowed hard. "I don't even know if she is pregnant. She hasn't taken the tests."

"She's pregnant," Besian said without hesitation. "I thought she looked different this morning, but just now, I was sure of it. I've seen plenty of pregnant women in my life. You have no idea how many dancers come into my office crying because their deadbeat boyfriends knocked them up again. It's in the face, the cheeks and eyes. Their movements are different. More careful, more guarded. She had her hand on her belly when we came through the door."

"I noticed," he admitted. His sole focus then had been to ensure her safety. Now, he didn't dare presume she might want what he wanted. "She might decide she isn't ready to be a mother yet."

Besian glared with disappointment. "If she makes that choice? To kill your baby? You fucking walk."

"I wasn't asking for your advice." He hated some of the harsh ideas Besian held. Fucking hated them. "You might end up on the pointy end of Marley's letter opener if you spew shit like that at her."

"That's done," Besian said harshly, turning his gaze out the window. "This was the second time she was nearly killed. The best thing that could happen to her is leaving this city forever."

"I don't think she wants to leave. Her whole life is here."

"I'm going to make sure Spider agrees with me and takes care of it. She has to go. She'll end up dead if she stays here."

"But, you both—," he tried to say.

"Drop it, Ben," Besian ordered roughly. "It's not happening."

He dropped it. There was nothing he could say that would change the boss's mind. Besian had seen Marley hurt twice now, and it seemed to be the breaking point. Whatever he had wanted with her, whatever he had envisioned with her, was gone. To protect her, Besian would push her away and work to exile her from the city.

In a way, Ben envied Besian's strength. Besian cared for Marley so much that he was willing to let her go to keep her safe. If he were a better man, he would have done the same with Aston.

But he wasn't.

His phone rang, startling him. Clearing his throat, he answered, "Hello?"

"Ben? It's Eric Santos. We found Aston and Marley."

"What! Where?" He played up his surprise. "Are they okay?"

"They're on their way to Methodist West on Katy Freeway."

"Okay. I'm headed that way."

"Ben?"

"Yeah?"

"You got lucky this time. Don't forget that."

"I won't." He slipped his phone into his pocket and glanced at Besian. "They're taking Aston and Marley to Methodist West."

"Go. Take care of them."

Hand on the door, he hesitated. "Are you sure you don't want to come?"

"I'm sure," Besian answered solemnly. "It's better this way."

Maybe it was.

CHAPTER SIXTEEN

"OW!" MARLEY HISSED and scowled at the paramedic digging a needle in her hand. "Third time better be the charm or else you're done jabbing needles in me."

"Sorry," he apologized. The tips of his ears were red with embarrassment. "I usually hit them on the first try."

"At least give me some of the good drugs," she insisted from the gurney. "You owe me a good time after all this."

Even though she was joking around, I knew that Marley was scared. After Kostya left and the police arrived and cleared the scene, we had been taken out to the waiting ambulance for assessment. Both of us had been hooked up to monitors to make sure the stun gun hadn't hurt our hearts. My strip showed absolutely no issues, but Marley's had caused the two paramedics on scene to exchange worried glances.

They tried to make me wait for a second ambulance to arrive, but Marley refused to get in without me. Desperate for her to get medical attention, I promised to sit quietly and not be a bother on the ride to the emergency room. Remembering that promise, I bit my tongue and stayed silent in my seat instead of asking the paramedic if it was really necessary to slide that needle that far into her hand. She was already bruising and had blood seeping along her skin and dripping onto the floor.

Thankfully, he managed to finally get the IV in place. He started running a bag of saline and checked her blood pressure and heart again. Anxiety twisted my stomach. What if the stun gun had permanently damaged her heart?

When she leaned her head back and got quiet, I knew she was really sick. She had gone a little pale and sweaty again, and suddenly, I was having flashbacks to the last few days of my father's life.

"Marley?" The paramedic touched her shoulder. "How you feeling?"

"Tired," she answered quietly. "Cold."

"Marley," the paramedic spoke loudly, his gaze fixed on the heart monitor and the spikes blipping across the screen, "is this the first time you've ever felt like this? Do you ever feel like you have some funny heartbeats? Feel like your heart is racing? Or too slow?"

She didn't answer for a few seconds. "It's not the first time," she admitted finally. "It started my sophomore year of college. The funny flip-flops and extra beats and racing. I thought it was just stress or too much caffeine and not enough sleep."

Squeezing my lips together, I held in my outburst. Why hadn't she said something before? Why had she been suffering all this time without telling me?

Because she never wants to be a burden.

Her entire life, Marley had felt like a burden to her mother, a professional martyr if I had ever seen one. Spider wasn't ever around long enough for her to ask for help. She always took care of herself. She wouldn't have wanted to worry me when I was dealing with my father dying. She had suffered in silence rather than be a bother. Realizing I had failed my best friend by taking more than I gave, I swore I would never, ever let her feel like she couldn't trust me with something so serious.

"Have you seen anyone about it?"

"No."

"And are you on any medications?"

"Just a vitamin and the occasional Tylenol or Motrin."

The paramedic looked concerned but not extremely worried as he watched the heart monitor screen and checked her vitals again. I tried to let his reactions guide mine. Maybe it seemed worse than it was. Maybe it wasn't so serious.

We reached the hospital finally, and I sagged with relief. I was vacillating between fear for the baby I was now certain I carried and my best friend. When I stepped out of the ambulance after Marley's gurney, I spotted Detectives Santos and Dawson waiting by the doors. *Are you kidding me?*

Before they could pester us, I held up a hand. "If you even try to ask Marley a question, I will spend every single penny I have making your lives miserable. She is absolutely off-limits. You can wait until I'm cleared and then I'll see you."

Both detectives looked at Marley's gurney and seemed to understand how sick she was. They nodded, and Eric said, "I'll have the nurse let me know when you're ready."

"Thank you." The detectives handled, I trailed after Marley until a nurse stopped me from going into the larger trauma room with her. Instead, she steered me into a different and smaller exam area.

"I don't want Marley to be alone."

"She has to undergo a full workup. You'll just be in the way right now. I'll check in with her nurse, and she'll let me know when you can see her. She'll have family on the way soon, I'm sure."

"Maybe," I said, not at all sure that her mother would answer the phone. I didn't even know if Spider was in the city or off traveling on club business.

She handed me a hospital gown and a paper bag. "The police want your clothing for evidence."

"All of it?"

"Yep."

"Okay."

"When you're done, go across the hall to the bathroom and fill this cup. There are posters in the stalls that explain how to do it correctly."

I took the urine specimen cup and the bag of supplies from her. "I'm pretty sure I'm pregnant."

"Fill 'er up and I'll let you know."

Alone in the curtained off exam room, I made quick work of removing my clothing and placing it in the bag. Every movement made me more aware of the bruising and sore muscles I had sustained. My underarm hurt the worst, and I winced when I discovered the raw burn marks there. *Fucking Gary.*

After a trip across the hall to the bathroom, I got up onto the exam table and curled onto my side. It was cold in the emergency room, and I used the paper-thin sheet to cover my trembling body.

"It's just shock," the nurse said gently when she returned. "You've been through a traumatic experience. Once you get something to eat and some rest, you'll feel better." She patted my hand. "And you're right. You are pregnant."

It seemed so anticlimactic to hear it from her. It wasn't the way I had envisioned learning I was pregnant. I had always imagined I would be nervously pacing my bathroom, not huddled on a hospital bed in a scratchy gown and cheap, threadbare sheet.

"Do you have any idea how far along you might be?"

"Um…" I thought back to my last period, not the spotting that I had mistaken for one. "Seven weeks?"

"Okay. I'm going to have one of our doctors come in and check those burns on your underarm. When they're done, we'll have an OB come in and do a scan. Have you ever been pregnant before?"

"No."

"Well, you're in good hands here, and we'll make sure that all of the testing we do today is sent to your OB/GYN." She patted my hand again. "Rest easy. Dr. Chavez will be in soon."

"What about Marley?"

"I'll check on her and let you know."

Curled on my side, I waited. The ER seemed busy with a constant stream of ambulance sirens echoing in the hallways. There were so many conversations happening all around me, the thin curtains providing no privacy. When Ben arrived, I would have to remember to keep my voice soft. I didn't want anyone eavesdropping on us.

When the curtain moved aside, I sat up hopefully, but it wasn't Ben. It was Dr. Chavez. She had a kind bedside manner and performed her exam quickly.

"Sorry," she apologized as she gently prodded the area

around the burn marks. "So, these are electrical burns, which, obviously, you knew. This one is partial thickness, but this one is more superficial. Your biggest concern will be keeping them clean and preventing an infection. We'll get you bandaged up, and I'll write a prescription for an ointment and an antibiotic. We'll also send you to a specialist for follow-up tomorrow. You will probably have more swelling and discomfort in the next day or so. Because you're pregnant, you'll need to stick to Tylenol for pain control."

Worried I wouldn't be able to remember all of that, I asked, "Will I get printed instructions?"

"Yes. Absolutely."

"Okay. Good."

The nurse returned to help clean and bandage my wounds. As she pulled on her gloves, she said, "Your friend's dad is on his way. Marley is going to be admitted, but visiting hours will be over by the time you're discharged. You'll have to wait to see her until tomorrow."

I didn't like it, but there wasn't anything I could do about it. Resigned to not seeing her again for a while, I turned on my side as Dr. Chavez instructed and winced as they dressed my burns. When they were done, I rolled onto my back but kept my arm up over my head because it was more comfortable. I heard the curtain open again but didn't lift my head, expecting the return of the nurse or the other doctor who was supposed to see me before I could be discharged.

"Miss McNeil? It's Detective Santos."

Grimacing at the ceiling, I sighed and sat up to face him. "Hello."

"I won't be long," he said, eyeing my bandaged arm as I

shrugged back into the gown and covered myself.

"It's fine. I'm still waiting to be seen by another doctor." Gripping the sheet, I asked, "Well?"

"Can you tell me what happened? Starting at Target," he guided.

"Marley and I were leaving Target, and I returned the cart. On the way back, I thought I saw someone in the minivan parked next to us, but I didn't think anything of it because, I mean, it's Target. When the door opened, it startled me, and I turned and he grabbed me."

"Gary Metcalfe?"

"Yes."

"How well did you know him?"

"Not well at all," I said truthfully. "I met him a few times at company parties. He didn't make much of an impression on me."

"You're close to his wife?"

"Close? I mean, we have a working relationship. I've known her for ten years or so. She's really nice and always takes the time to answer questions and teach. She's not a close friend, but she's a friend."

"What happened after Gary stunned you? Do you remember anything?"

"No. I passed out, and when I woke up, I was throwing up in that office. Marley was behind me, and we both had our wrists and ankles tied up with those plastic cord things."

"Zipties?"

"Yeah."

"And what happened after you woke up?"

"Marley was really mad, and she yelled at Gary that we

needed water. She looked off to me," I said, picturing her clearly in my mind. "She was sweating and shaky. I could tell that she was sick."

"They told me they're admitting her to the cardiac unit," Eric confirmed. "I guess they're trying to figure out if the stun gun caused her heart problems or aggravated a pre-existing condition."

I rubbed my face, hating the thought of Marley alone and scared somewhere in the hospital. "Did you see Spider?"

"Not yet," he said, "but they told me he's on his way."

"Please, Detective, don't bother Marley with this," I begged. "She doesn't need the stress."

"As long as I get all the answers I need from you, I'll leave her alone," he promised. "What happened next in the office building?"

"Gary came back with water. He cleaned up my face with some paper towels. He helped me sit up and then hauled Marley over to sit next to me. He started talking, started telling us about the scam he was running with Calvin."

"What was the scam?"

"Real estate," I said, deciding to be careful with the details. "He didn't get into the nitty gritty of it, but I think it was money laundering."

"For the Triad?"

Realizing Eric knew far more than he was letting on, I nodded. "That's what he said."

"Did he mention Paul Chen?"

"He did. I'm not sure exactly what his part was in their scheme."

"Do you know why Gary's wife and baby were kidnapped?"

"Calvin ran off without sharing the accounts with Gary or Paul. They couldn't get their hands on the money they owed their Chinese investors so they started taking it from Gary's legitimate clients. When that well ran dry, they couldn't meet their obligations."

"That squares with what we've worked out," Eric said, scribbling something on the small notepad he had taken from his pocket.

"Did they find them?"

"Who?"

"Margie and Elliot," I clarified, hoping that Teddy Leung hadn't double-crossed me.

"Yes. They're safe and on their way to a hospital downtown."

I exhaled with relief. "Thank God."

"I'm not sure God had anything to do with it," Eric muttered. "I have a feeling someone paid a hefty ransom for them."

"Wouldn't you?" I leveled a knowing gaze at him.

"Yeah," he said after a moment's pause. "I would."

"I thought they were dead," I added, thinking of the moment when the elevator had opened. "When Marley and I were trying to fight off Gary and escape, the elevator dinged, and we heard men yelling. I figured they had already killed Margie and her baby and were coming to finish us all off."

"You got lucky," Eric remarked. "You saw what they did to Gary."

"We didn't see it exactly," I replied. "We heard it. We were already running at that point."

"You two stabbed him before he got shot?"

I nodded. "Marley found a letter opener and a pair of scissors in the desk in the room where he was holding us. We decided our best chance was to fight."

"You were right. It's always better to fight." He clicked his pen a few times. "How did you get free?"

"From the zipties?"

"Yes."

"I lied to him."

"About?"

"About helping him get back Margie and Elliot."

"I see."

"I didn't know what else to try," I said with a shrug.

"He believed you?"

"He did. He cut us loose and went to find a phone so he could contact the kidnappers. Marley found the weapons, and we attacked him when he came back."

"And then the gang got there?"

"Yeah, and we ran. We tried to get out of the building, but the door was locked. Marley spotted some men outside, and we realized it was more of the Chinese mafia guys. We ran back upstairs, tried to find somewhere to hide and ended up in the supply room behind the boxes of paper. We heard more gunshots and more men in the building. After a while, it got quiet, and we left the supply closet and found Gary's phone. I called 9-1-1 and the rest you know."

I repeated the story we had rehearsed with the terrifying Russian. He had been very clear that we needed to never mention him or any of Ben's crew.

"You didn't see the men who shot Gary?"

"No."

"You're sure they were Triad?"

"How would I be able to tell? All I know is that they were speaking Cantonese."

His brow furrowed. "You can tell the difference in dialect?"

"Only a little bit," I said. "Dad put me in Mandarin classes when I was a kid, but I really struggled with it. They switched me over to Cantonese, and I still couldn't get it. I know what I heard—and it was Cantonese."

He scribbled another note. "Is there anything else you can remember?"

"I don't think so."

"You don't remember making a 9-1-1 call about Margie and her baby being in danger?"

He was smooth. I had to give him that. He'd slipped in that question without any indication that he was going there.

Looking him square in the eye, I lied. "I made the call."

"I see."

"Do you?"

"Were they threatening you? The Triad?"

It was the easiest thing to agree to and kept the focus off of Ben and my betrayal. "Yes."

"You were worried they would go after Margie?"

"Yes."

"Next time, just call me. I can help you."

"There won't be a next time."

"There will," he said with a resigned sigh. "If you remember anything or if you hear from Calvin, contact me." He handed me a business card from the back of his little notebook.

"I will." I definitely would not.

"I hope you feel better soon."

"Thanks."

He hesitated at the curtain. "About last night? At your place?"

I shook my head. "Don't worry about it. I know you're just trying to do your job."

Eric nodded and left the exam room. Not even five seconds later, Ben finally appeared. He crossed the distance between us with quick, powerful strides and wrapped his arms around me. We had hugged and kissed earlier, but without the adrenaline and fear surging through me, I sagged against him. He smelled so good, and his body heat soothed my raw nerves. He kissed my cheek and my neck and then my mouth, his lips lingering on mine while his fingers combed through my hair.

Foreheads pressed together, we stared into each other's eyes. This wasn't the way I wanted to tell him, but there was no reason to wait. He needed to know.

"Ben," I said, pulling back so I could see him better, "I'm pregnant."

He smiled lovingly and brushed his thumbs over my cheeks. "I know."

"What? How?"

"They found two pregnancy tests in your bags at Target. I was sure they weren't Marley's."

"No, they were for me." I swallowed anxiously. "Are you...? I mean... How do you feel about it?"

"How do *you* feel about it?"

Frowning, I insisted, "I asked first."

"Fine." He huffed out a little laugh. "I feel excited and happy and scared and worried. It's a lot to take in, you know?"

"I know," I assured him. "I know. I feel the same way. Just a jumble of emotions."

"Good or bad?"

"Mostly good," I said, feeling shy as I added, "and I really want to keep the baby."

"So do I," he said, his whole body visibly relaxing. "I don't want to pressure you, and if you change your mind—"

"I'm not changing my mind," I interrupted with certainty. "I want our baby."

This time, Ben kissed me so tenderly it brought tears to my eyes. Ever so gently, he placed his hand on my stomach. "We made a baby."

"We did." I covered his hand with my own and kissed him. "We're going to be parents."

"I don't know the first thing about being a dad."

"I don't know the first thing about being a mom," I replied, thinking of how my mother had failed me. "We'll figure it out, Ben."

He nodded, but didn't get a chance to answer as the obstetrician finally arrived. She introduced herself before pulling on a pair of gloves. My nurse came back with a portable ultrasound machine and pulled the stirrups into place. I glanced at Ben who had suddenly turned his attention to the ceiling, and I couldn't help but smile at his discomfort. Who would have thought he would be embarrassed by a pair of stirrups?

Once the doctor had the uncomfortable probe inserted, Ben finally lowered his gaze, first to my face and then to the ultrasound screen. I wasn't quite sure what I was supposed to see in the fuzzy black and white image. Thankfully, the doctor pointed out my cervix and uterus to help us understand what we were looking at in that moment.

"And here it is," she said with a bright smile. "Your baby."

Ben interlaced our fingers and squeezed tight. I glanced at his face, but he was entranced by the image on the screen. He looked stunned and scared but then his mouth curved with happiness. He grinned down at me and mouthed, "I love you."

Eyes stinging with tears, I watched the little white peanut floating in its black bubble. It was surreal to think that our baby was growing inside me. The fast blips of its heartbeat reassured me that all was well. Rendered almost speechless by the sight of our baby, I could barely muster any response to the doctor's questions.

When the doctor and nurse left, Ben and I stared at the printed strip of ultrasound pictures. He traced the tiny baby and said, "Can you believe we made this?"

"We're pretty good at this baby making thing," I teased. "We didn't even have to try."

Ben laughed and kissed me. Ignoring the buzz of the emergency room, we shared our sweet moment, just the two of us dazzled by the possibilities of our future. It was a moment I never wanted to end.

CHAPTER SEVENTEEN

Six Weeks Later

"**A**RE YOU SURE you have everything? Passport? Credit cards? Cash? Backup cash? Phone? The right SIM card? The different battery charger?"

"Yes, Mother!" Marley answered with a sarcastic laugh as she grabbed her seatbelt and fastened it. "I checked and rechecked my list. I'm ready."

"Okay." I glanced at my mirrors before pulling away from her house. "Did you want to stop by your mom's place?"

"No." Her tone communicated that she was absolutely done with her mom's bullshit.

Not wanting to upset her by asking what her mom had done this time, I simply nodded. "Spider?"

"I saw him last night."

"Has he calmed down about your trip? Or is he still going bananas trying to convince you to stay?"

"He was the one who told me I needed to get out of Houston," she replied bitterly. "If he wants me gone, I'm going far away."

"Not for good," I interjected selfishly. "Right?"

"No, just to clear my head," she said. "I promise I will be back in time to plan and host your baby shower."

"You better! I can't have this baby without Aunt Marley right next to me."

"You'll have plenty of support with Grandma Nina and Grandpa Pedro," she insisted. "You know, once they let go of their vendetta against Ben for knocking you up."

"Oh, don't remind me," I grumbled, thinking of the absolute shit show in our kitchen when I told them. Not even Ben's expert handling of the broken lawn mower had soothed Pedro's ire. Nina has been on the verge of a breakdown as she cried about disappointing my dad by letting me run wild.

"When are they coming back to town?"

"Next week." Smiling at Marley as we slowed to a stop for a red light, I added, "Nina sent me pics of some onesies she picked up in Maui. They're adorable."

"I guess she's forgiven you."

"Hopefully."

"They love you," Marley said gently. "They only want what's best for you."

"I know." After the initial hysterics, we had sat down and discussed things like adults. Pedro had been relieved that I wanted to sell the house and downsize. Nina had been surprisingly enthusiastic about my decision and revealed she had been dreaming about finally traveling to all the places on her bucket list. They weren't thrilled that I was going to be an unwed mother or that my relationship with Ben was still so new, but they had wished us the best. It was all I could hope for at the time. Eventually, they would come around.

My phone buzzed in the cup holder between us. "Can you check that?"

"Sure." She picked it up and read the screen. "Ben wants to

know what MAWICL means?"

"Master Walk-In Closet," I explained, shaking my head. "He was standing right next to me when we labeled those boxes."

"You were probably bending over and showing him your ass or those ginormous pregnancy tatas," she reasoned as she answered the text. "He was using the wrong head."

I snickered. "Probably."

"Has that gotten any better? The whole afraid to touch you thing?"

"Much better," I said, blushing at the memory of tying him down again and having my way with him. "He's finally accepted that he can't break me or hurt the baby."

"Good."

"*Very* good."

My phone buzzed again, and Marley snorted before reading it aloud. "Are you texting and driving?"

I rolled my eyes. "Are there, like, twenty exclamation marks?"

"Yep." She tapped at the screen. "I told him it's me." A few seconds later she said, "Aww," she said. "Look, he's already acting like a father!"

"Is he giving you the stranger danger talk?"

"Yep." She put my phone back in the cup holder. "He's going to be a good dad."

"Definitely," I agreed. My gaze drifted to one of the billboards along the interstate. It was matte black with a big, ripe peach grasped in a man's hand. The glistening flesh and dripping juice communicated exactly what they were supposed to: sex.

"Well, that's an attention getter," Marley remarked, her gaze glued to the risqué billboard. "Peaches? That's what they decided to call the new club?"

"It's less gross than Wet," I replied, wrinkling my nose at the name of one of Besian's other clubs.

"Almost classy," she said with a giggle.

"Almost." As I took the exit for the airport, I decided it was now or never. Carefully, I asked, "Have you heard from him at all?"

"No," she said softly, sadly. "When he didn't visit me in the hospital, I knew." Her gaze drifted to the window. "I thought maybe he would come see me at my last shift at the pawn shop, but..."

"I'm sorry."

"Don't be. It's not as if we ever actually dated." She trailed her finger over the dash. "It wasn't ever real. It was just a whisper of something that might have been."

I smiled at her description. "You should write while you're on your trip. You have such a beautiful way with words, Marley."

"I'll think about it."

Following the signs to Terminal D, I asked, "Are you sure you feel up to this?"

"I'm fine," she insisted. "They zapped my heart. I'm taking my meds. I'm good."

Not long after she had been admitted, the cardiac team had diagnosed her with a heart defect. Wolff-Parkinson-White Syndrome. She'd been born with extra electrical pathways. The cardiac team had decided a catheter ablation was the best option for treating the problem. So far, she seemed better, and

I had to trust that she was telling the truth about being healthy enough to explore Europe on her own.

Slowing to a stop in the unloading lane, I put my Jeep in park and hit the hazards. I flipped down the visor and retrieved the airplane ticket I had stored there. Handing it over, I said, "Happy early birthday."

She frowned. "What's this?"

"Your ticket to London."

"But, Spider said—"

"I convinced him to let me buy your plane tickets."

"Aston!" she gasped after opening the ticket sleeve. "You are not serious!"

"Like I'm letting my best friend fly to London in coach?"

"First class? British Airways! It's too much."

"It's not. You deserve it."

With happy tears in her eyes, she reached across the console and hugged me. "I'm going to miss the hell out of you."

"Promise me you'll call or FaceTime me every day."

"I will." Reluctantly, she pulled back. "I better go."

"You want me to help you with your suitcase?"

She shook her head. "I got it."

I felt like a mother bird watching her baby bird jump from the nest as Marley gathered up her backpack and suitcase. She smiled as she closed the door and waved from the sidewalk. I waited until a porter grabbed her bag to turn off my hazards and ease into the traffic flowing through the departures terminal. I had to remind myself not to take my usual exit at the airport. Our new house was easier to reach if I used the Hardy toll road.

Our new house.

The thought thrilled me. We had closed on our new place last week and were moving in today. The freshly renovated house in the Heights wasn't anything like we had envisioned as our first home together. After touring a dozen model homes and a handful of luxury apartments, we hadn't found a single place we both liked.

Then, Ben had called one morning and asked to pick me up for lunch. He had surprised me with a side trip to see an older house that had come onto the market that morning. We hadn't considered the Heights during our initial searches, and the house was older and bigger than we had wanted. I was skeptical until the house came into view.

It looked like the set of a Hallmark movie with its wraparound porch, gated yard and carriage house. Even though the exterior was love at first sight, I was worried the interior would disappoint. I couldn't have been more wrong. The home had been beautifully renovated. Walking through each room, I had no problem imagining our little family living there.

Our offer was submitted and accepted that same day. Tonight would be our first in the new house. Knowing Ben had been handling the movers while I spent time with Marley, I made a detour to Phan's.

They had been open almost two weeks in their new and slightly larger location. The line of diehard pho fans was out the door when I arrived. Certain it was worth the wait, I joined the queue and swiped my phone screen.

For a Friday, my work inbox seemed almost empty. There was a reminder from Oliver's PA about a meeting on Monday afternoon and another from the building supervisor about the resurfacing of the parking lot. My gaze flicked down to the message from Margie, and I hesitated before opening it.

The message was nothing more than a lighthearted selfie of Margie and Elliot taken on the London Eye. She looked happy in it, more relaxed and well-rested. Elliot's chubby little face was just as bright and adorable as ever.

I hadn't gone to Gary's funeral. I hadn't wanted to be a distraction or cause unnecessary gossip or drama. I waited almost a week before asking if I could visit her. She had graciously invited me over for coffee. I hadn't stayed long, and the visit was awkward. She seemed to hint that she knew I had paid the ransom, but I didn't want or need to be thanked.

After the nightmare she had survived, Margie had decided she wanted a fresh start. Jed still wanted to let her go, but I had squared up with him over it and made the case to Oliver that the firm had invested more than a decade with her. She was an asset. We had to keep her. In the end, Oliver had offered her a promotion and position at the London headquarters of StrateCore. Her mother had moved with her, and it seemed they weren't likely to come back.

As I neared the front of the line, my phone buzzed with a new text message. I recognized the number and grimaced. *Teddy Leung.*

Ever since we'd met to exchange the crypto, he had been sending flirtatious messages. Ben wasn't amused by them, but I had explained this was just alpha male bullshit. Teddy wanted to agitate him. He had promised me that he wouldn't let it bother him, and I had promised that I would share the messages with him for full transparency. I had considered blocking Teddy's number, but Ben had been sure Teddy would find another way to bother me. Text messages I could handle.

Leaving the message on read, I dropped my phone in my handbag and pulled out my wallet. I ordered Ben's favorite for both of us and moved down the busy line to pay. Dinner in hand, I left the restaurant and strolled back to my Jeep.

When I slid behind the wheel, I was reminded of the cargo I now carried. Almost fourteen weeks now, I couldn't hide my condition. The swell of my stomach was more prominent, and my preferred styles did little to camouflage it. Not that I wanted to hide it. Once I had reached the end of my first trimester, I felt comfortable enough to let everyone know.

"Ben? I'm home!" I called out as I walked into our kitchen. "I stopped at Phan's."

When he didn't answer, I toed off my shoes, left dinner on the counter and set off to find him. In the living room, I was taken aback by a giant flower arrangement and two bottles adorned with bright pink bows. Curious, I checked the card and smiled.

Congratulations on the new house! Here's a bottle for now and another for later! Love, Alina

I looked at the labels. One was non-alcoholic champagne and the other a very expensive bottle of Louis Roederer. Touched by her considerate housewarming gifts, I carried them both back to the kitchen. The non-alcoholic bottle I stowed in the freezer to enjoy after dinner.

"Ben?" I called out again as I headed upstairs.

"I'm in the nursery."

My heart did a funny little flip. Ben had picked out the room next to ours for the nursery. He had already been sketching plans to open the wall between the two with French doors to make it easier to get to the baby at night.

When I walked into the nursery, I found Ben taping paint swatches to the walls. The colors varied from soft pastels in shades of pink and blue and yellow to deeper, richer hues of green and gray.

"Hey," he greeted with a smile. "Marley make it to her flight on time?"

"She did."

"Come here." He held out his hand, and I grasped it, letting him draw me into his embrace. He kissed me, the touch of his lips tender but promising more heat later. When he drew back, he asked, "What do you think?"

Snuggling in close to him, I studied the colors he had chosen. "I expected to prefer the pastels, but I think I actually like the darker colors better."

"Same," he agreed. "I looked on Pinterest—"

"You looked on Pinterest," I interrupted, shocked. "*You*?"

"Be nice." He pinched my butt, and I squealed and swatted away his hand. "I asked Marley where to find nursery ideas. She told me to download the app, and we started sharing a board."

"You sneaks!"

He laughed and patted my bottom. "You can have the link to our board."

"If?" I sensed there was some quid pro quo to the offer.

"We can negotiate later."

"Uh-huh." I moved out of his arms and walked over to the stack of old, dusty boxes in the corner. "What are these?"

"Alina brought them with the flowers and champagne." Ben followed me and placed a reverent hand on the top box.

"They were my mom's. Or, I guess, they're mine. My baby stuff and toys. Alina thought I would want them."

"Oh, Ben, that's so sweet!"

"I don't know if any of it is usable," he cautioned.

"Even if it's not, we can always choose a few things to display in here. Make little shadow boxes or something like that," I decided, my brain already conjuring up ideas. "Did you have any more trouble with our boxes?"

"Just one," he said, sweeping my hair off my shoulder and pressing a delicate kiss to my neck.

I leaned into his touch. "What does the label say?"

"It wasn't labeled."

"Then you must have packed it because I labeled all of my boxes."

"I think you're right." He shifted in front of me. "It's this one."

My gaze fell to the small black box in his hand before darting right back to his smiling, hopeful face. "Ben?"

"I had planned to do this somewhere more romantic, but it feels right to do it here, in our house, in the room for our baby."

"Ben," I whispered, crying now.

He carefully opened the box to reveal a classic and very simple emerald cut solitaire on a platinum band. It was exactly what I would have chosen, not too fussy or gaudy. In short, it was perfect.

"It's beautiful, Ben."

"Will you marry me?" he asked, his voice thick with emotion. "Will you let me be your husband? Your partner?"

"Yes! To all of it!" Unable to contain my happiness, I

threw my arms around his neck and excitedly kissed him. "Ben, I love you so much."

"I love you more," he murmured against my mouth. His hand drifted between us and settled over the gentle swell of my stomach. "I love you both."

Safe in Ben's arms, I leaned my cheek against his chest and listened to the familiar thud of his heartbeat. Our first night in our house, and we were already making beautiful, joyous memories. I couldn't wait to see what new wonders tomorrow would bring...

The End.

Also by Roxie Rivera

Her Russian Protector
Ivan
Dimitri
Yuri
Nikolai
Sergei
Sergei 2
Nikolai 2
Kostya
Alexei

Fighting Connollys
In Kelly's Corner
In Jack's Arms
In Finn's Heart

Debt Collection
Collateral
Collateral 2

About the Author

A *New York Times* and *USA Today* bestselling author, I like to write super sexy romances and scorching hot erotica. I live in Texas on five acres with my husband, two daughters and our wild and ever-expanding menagerie of pets.

You can find me online at www.roxierivera.com.

CHAPTER ONE

*B*zzzz. *B*zzzz. *B*zzzz.

With a groan, I slapped the bedside table, knocking the Series 82 study guide onto the floor as I blindly searched for my phone. When I found it, I opened one eye and turned my bleary gaze to the screen. When the buzzing sound continued, I realized it wasn't my phone ringing. "Ben?"

He grunted behind me and shifted closer. "Let it ring."

"It's been ringing for a while."

With another grunt and a flex of his muscled forearm, he dragged me closer. He buried his face in my hair. "Whatever it is can wait. Go back to sleep."

It was easy enough with his body heat radiating through me. Safe in his arms, I dozed for a little while longer until the insistent vibrations finally cut through the sleepy haze. I shifted away from Ben, but his arm tightened. "Stay," he all but ordered.

"It's almost time for my alarm." I raised his scarred, rough hand and pressed a gentle kiss on it. "You stay. Get some more sleep."

Eventually, I managed to extricate myself, but not before Ben tried to coax me back with teasingly soft kisses and the slow caress of his hands. Rubbing my face, I walked around the bed and stumbled over the unexpected pile of clothes he had dropped there the night prior. With a frown, I crouched down to pick them up. We were still in the early phase of our relationship, and I didn't want to nag about his untidy habits but...

"Ben, there's a hamper in the bathroom."

"Sorry," he said, his voice raspy from sleep. "I was dead on my feet when I got in last night."

Judging by the filthy state of his clothes, he had been working hard at his shop. The pocket of his jeans started to vibrate, and I fished his phone out of it. A glance at the screen showed dozens of missed calls and texts. Concerned, I brought the phone back to the bed and gave his shoulder a little shake. "Ben? I think you need to answer this."

With a deep inhale, he stretched his arms overhead and groaned. Every muscle in his chest and abdomen rippled as he moved. Even after all the times I had run my greedy hands over him, I still couldn't believe he was all mine.

"Come here." He grasped the front of my tee and tugged me down for a possessive kiss. "I'm sorry I'm such a slob." His hand slid down my side until he cupped by bottom and gave it a squeeze. "The next time I make a mess you can spank me."

I giggled at his lascivious smile and kissed him. "Pervert."

"Baby, I grew up in a brothel. What do you expect?"

"You're terrible." I gently swatted him. "Check your messages. I have to get ready for work."

"I have a better idea." He snatched my hand. "Let's stay in bed."

"I can't."

"Call in sick." He pulled me closer and started dotting

ticklish kisses up my arm. "You own the place."

"Not exactly," I countered, trying to ignore the flare of need that beat low in my belly. It wasn't hard to imagine his soft mouth placing kisses somewhere else. "It's a complex legal situation with a trust and a board and—oh!"

He had finally reached the sensitive curve of my neck. Thankfully, I was saved from completely surrendering to his talented mouth by his phone ringing again. He growled with irritation and abandoned his attempted seduction. I kissed his cheek and backed away from the bed as he picked up his phone and swiped his thumb over the screen.

I was standing at the sink, brushing my teeth, when I heard him shout. Wondering what was wrong, I opened the bathroom door and found him hopping back into his dirty jeans. As my toothbrush vibrated in my hand, I listened to his end of the conversation and grew increasingly worried.

"Is he okay? Which hospital? Yeah. Yeah. I'm on my way." He shoved his phone into his back pocket and glanced around for his shirt.

"What happened?"

He plopped down on the edge of the bed to put on his boots. "Two of our guys transporting the cash from a private poker game got hit last night. The car was totaled. One of them is in the hospital. The other is banged up."

"Was it a drunk driver?"

He shook his head. "It was a robbery. They slammed into our guys, stole all the cash and left."

My stomach clenched with fear. Ben's life as an enforcer and street soldier in the local Albanian outfit wasn't foreign to me. It was something I had accepted about him. I didn't like it, but I had accepted it as the price of having him in my life. "Was it a lot of money?"

Ben looked up in surprise. "That was not the question I expected you to ask."

"I'm fully aware of what you do, Ben. There's no point in me asking you not to go track down the thief and do whatever it is you do to people who steal from you." I shrugged and jammed my toothbrush back in my mouth.

He grinned. "You sound like an old school mob wife."

Laughing, I finished brushing my teeth. Thinking about the clique of beautiful mob wives who could often be found visiting the salon I loved, I joked, "Maybe I'll get to hang out with the cool girls at Allure now."

"I'm surprised you're not all friends already," he admitted, lacing up his boots. "You went to the same prep school, right?"

"Different years," I explained, still standing in the doorway of the bathroom. "We're having an alumni thing in a few months. Maybe I'll reintroduce myself."

"You should. They'd be lucky to have you as a friend."

His sweet remark left me smiling sappily. My smile faded as he stood and crossed the distance between us. He placed his hands on my hips and nuzzled my cheek. "I really am sorry that I came home late and am already running out the door."

"It's okay." I looped my arms around his broad shoulders. "Do you think you'll be home for dinner? Nina is cooking, remember?"

He made a face. "She hates me, Aston."

I rolled my eyes. "She doesn't hate you. She just doesn't know you yet."

"She threatened to send her nephews after me," he retorted. "Diego? I can take him. Nate? I'll end up in the ICU if I'm on the business end of his fists."

"Nate and Diego are the nicest guys. They would never beat you up!"

"Says the girl who has never been to an underground cage fight," he countered. "You know what they call those two? The Kings of Coronado Street. They control a huge piece of the Houston underworld. So, yeah, when she says she'll send her nephews after me? I believe her."

Patting his chest, I sighed. "I'll talk to her, but *you* have to make an effort. Come to dinner. Be nice. Show her all the reasons I love you."

"I'm pretty sure she'd have me arrested if I showed her the things you love most about me."

I rolled my eyes even harder. "*That* is not the thing I love most about you."

"You sure? Because last night..."

I hushed him with a kiss and punctuated each word with one. "Go. Handle. Your. Business."

"I really want to handle you," he said, his big hands cupping my backside.

"Later." I kissed him again. "Go."

"I'll try to make it back in time for dinner. I'll message you."

"Don't forget to pick up your tux."

"Shit. I forgot all about the wedding." He winced. "I'm not sure I'll have time..."

I sighed. "Fine. I'll get it."

"Thank you." He caressed my cheek before stepping away. "I'll see you tonight."

"Be careful, Ben."

"I always am." He lingered in the doorway of my bed-room. "I really do love you, Aston."

My heart thumped wildly. "I love you, too."

After he was gone, I marveled at the way his words made me feel. We were still in that period of our relationship where everything was new, bright and exciting. Things were moving fast—maybe too fast—but I couldn't seem to pump the brakes. Everything about us worked. We had clicked on a level I had never experienced, and I couldn't imagine not spending every free moment with him.

But as I stepped into the shower and tried to mentally prep for the day ahead, I couldn't shake the nagging worry that Ben was walking straight into danger.

CHAPTER TWO

B EN HATED HOSPITALS. The smell, the lights, the squeaky tile floors—they brought him straight back to the worst months of his mother's life. Watching her fight through the surgeries and the chemo and then through those last agonizing days of pain…

Stretching his neck, he tried to push away those ugly memories. He found his way to the room where Agim was resting. He eyed the uniformed cop leaning against the nurse's station. The cop was too busy flirting with the pretty brunette to notice him slipping into Agim's room.

"Ags?" Ben gently called to his friend. Agim had mostly stayed out of trouble and avoided working with the family. He'd just finished his engineering degree and was working for an oil and gas firm. Unfortunately, he had student loans and running pickups and drop-offs was the easiest way to earn extra money.

"Ben." Agim winced as he spoke. His mouth looked terrible, both lips were split and the skin around them was already a deep maroon with bruising. His nose was broken and one eye was swollen shut. His left arm was elevated and in a cast. "Looks worse than it is."

"I don't know, Ags. It looks pretty fucking bad." He sat in

the chair next to the bed. "I won't bother you for long. The boss wanted me to come by and see if you had any information that can help me track down the cash."

"I didn't see the guys who hit us. I was driving. My focus was on traffic. I heard Aleks shout, and a second later, we were rolling. I woke up in the back of an ambulance. That's…that's all I remember."

"Aleks told the boss that he saw a red truck coming up behind you. The truck accelerated and got into the left lane to pass you." Ben used his hands to illustrate the movements Aleks had described. "He said the guy hit you in a pit maneuver. You lost control. The car started to flip. Aleks blacked out for a minute or less. When he came around, a guy was taking the cash bag from the backseat. He didn't see his face. The robber was wearing gloves, and he didn't speak." He waited a few seconds, giving Ags a chance to digest what he had described. "Did you or Aleks tell anyone about the route you were taking? Did you tell anyone you were picking up the money?"

"No, I didn't tell anyone."

"Okay."

"But…"

"But?"

"I, uh, I driver the same route every time I do the poker game pickup," Ags admitted.

"Ags," Ben said and exhaled roughly. "You know the fucking rules."

"Yeah. I know. I *know*. But—m"

"But?"

"It's late, and I work all day. I'm tired, you know? It's just easier to take the same route every time."

"Besian is going to backhand the dog piss out of you when you get out of here," Ben warned.

"If I'm lucky, that's all he'll do." Ags stared at his hand as if imagining it with a few less fingers. Another thought seemed to trouble him. "You think it was an inside job?"

"I sure as hell hope not," Ben replied.

"I figure it was either someone who played the game and knew the location or someone who works with us or for us. How else would they know to follow me?"

Ben had been thinking the same thing. "It could be a rival gang."

"Tracking that money down is going to keep you busy."

"That's what the boss pays me to do." Ben rose from his chair. "Get some rest."

"I will."

Ben hesitated by the door. "Do you have someone coming? I can send someone to sit with you."

"My mom is on her way," Ags explained, looking chagrined. "She's really pissed off."

"Of course, she is. How many times did she tell you not to hang out with us?"

"Too many."

"She's probably going to ground you for a month."

Ags coughed out a short laugh before groaning. "Get out of here. If she gets here before you leave, she's liable to hit you with her purse."

Certain that Mrs. Shrkeli would beat his ass if she got hands on him, Ben hightailed it out of the hospital. Agim's information matched what Aleks had told them, but it wasn't helpful. A red truck? There were hundreds of those in the greater Houston area.

While he waited for an elevator, he texted Besian asking for a meeting place. By the time he made it to his motorcycle in the nearby parking garage, he had his answer. Ben thought it was a little strange to meet the boss at a bookstore, but it definitely wasn't the weirdest place they'd ever met. A funeral home, a garbage dump, a trap house, a meat packing plant—yeah. There had definitely been stranger places than a small, neighborhood bookstore.

It definitely got weirder once he found the boss browsing the shelves in the nonfiction section. Always immaculately dressed in a suit and tie, Besian looked right at home in the store, but it was jarring for Ben to find one of Houston's most ruthless mob bosses flicking through the pages of a book on feminist theory.

Recognizing one of the books Besian held, Ben said, "You could always just borrow Aston's copy of that one."

Besian narrowed his eyes, silently warning Ben not to fuck with him about the books he was buying. He added a copy of *The Second Sex* to his growing stack. "I like to read different subjects. I haven't ever read any of these."

"Uh-huh." Ben had a pretty good idea why Besian was suddenly so interested in this section of the store. A certain pretty little pawn shop cashier happened to have a degree in the field. "You should probably take a Xanax before you start reading those."

"I'm not a misogynist," Besian insisted.

"You should pick up a dictionary for your stack," Ben suggested. "Look it up. Your face is right next to it."